Praise for *Small Change for Stuart*

'A book full of warmth, sharp humour and clever puzzles'
Patrick Ness, *Time Out*

'One of this year's great delights . . . It's a finely written book
crammed with exciting incident and colourful characters;
something quite special' *Independent on Sunday*

'A wonderfully intriguing adventure' *Daily Telegraph*

Praise for *Big Change for Stuart*

'A gem for budding heroes' *The Times*

'It delivers everything a good old-fashioned adventure
should . . . A smart book for a smart young reader'
Marcus Sedgwick, *Guardian*

'A story fluctuating between humour and high drama . . .
The first story about this likeable boy, published last year,
came out to universal praise. This second one is just as good'
Independent on Sunday

www.randomhousechildrens.co.uk

About the Author

This is Lissa's second book for Random House Children's Publishers. Her first, *Small Change for Stuart*, was shortlisted for the Carnegie Medal, the Costa Children's Book Award, the UKLA Children's Book Award and the Branford Boase Award, and longlisted for the Guardian Children's Book Award. She has also written books for adults and younger children. After a brief career in medicine, and then in stand-up comedy, Lissa became a comedy producer, first for radio and then in television. She lives with her family in north London.

BIG CHANGE FOR STUART

BY LISSA EVANS

Interior illustrations by Temujin Doran

CORGI BOOKS

BIG CHANGE FOR STUART
A CORGI BOOK 978 0 552 56195 2

First published in Great Britain by Doubleday,
an imprint of Random House Children's Publishers UK
A Random House Group Company

Hardback edition published 2012
This edition published 2013

5 7 9 10 8 6

Text copyright © Lissa Evans, 2012
Interior illustrations copyright © Temujin Doran, 2012
Cover illustration copyright © David Dean, 2013

Set in Minion Regular

Corgi Books are published by Random House Children's Publishers UK,
61–63 Uxbridge Road, London W5 5SA

www.**randomhousechildrens**.co.uk
www.**totallyrandombooks**.co.uk
www.**randomhouse**.co.uk

Addresses for companies within The Random House Group Limited
can be found at: www.randomhouse.co.uk/offices.htm

THE RANDOM HOUSE GROUP Limited Reg. No. 954009

A CIP catalogue record for this book is available from the British Library.

Penguin Random House is committed to a sustainable future for
our business, our readers and our planet. This book is made from
Forest Stewardship Council® certified paper.

MIX
Paper from
responsible sources
FSC® C018179

Printed and bound in Great Britain by Clays Ltd, Elcograf S.p.A.

For my mum
Who read like the wind
and loved books
And who was always the
first to read mine

Chapter 1

Stuart Horten sat at the kitchen table and looked at the front page of the crummy little newspaper he'd just been given. Then, with a feeling of foreboding, he began to read.

THE BEECH ROAD GUARDIAN
Exclusive!!!

Beech Road resident (Stuart Horten, aged 10, but looks younger) discovers his lost great - uncle's hidden magician's workshop under the bandstand in Beeton park!!

Stuart Horten (10, but looks younger) moved to Beeton at the start of the summer holidays, less than a month ago, but already claims to have made a huge discovery. His great-uncle, Tony Horten (known as 'Teeny-tiny Tony Horten' because he was very short), was a famous stage magician who disappeared in 1944, leaving the whereabouts of his workshop unknown.

It turns out that it is in a huge underground room beneath the bandstand in Beeton Park. This was revealed during last week's Beeton Festival children's talent contest, when the floor of the bandstand gave way while a group of ballet students was performing. Stuart admits that the collapse of the floor was his fault, because he turned an underground wheel 'by accident'.

Stuart claims that he 'worked out' where the workshop was by 'following clues' — though he refuses to tell the Beech Road Guardian what those clues were. He also claims ownership of the contents of the workshop, which consist of various tools and workbenches, and a selection of magic tricks used in his great-uncle's stage act. 'They are definitely mine,' claims Stuart. 'My great-uncle left them to me.'

When asked if he could prove this in any way, he thought for a bit, and then admitted he couldn't.

Beeton Museum has agreed to give a temporary home to the contents of the workshop. The curator, Rod Felton, said, 'This is an exciting discovery for Beeton. Though not quite as exciting as if it had been some kind of Roman weapon, like a ballista.'

Stuart (10, but looks younger) claims that—

'Why do your sisters keep writing that?' asked Stuart indignantly.

'Keep writing what?' asked his friend and next-door neighbour, April Kingley, who'd brought him the paper. 'You mean *ten, but looks younger*?'

'No. The word *claims*. *Stuart claims this, Stuart claims that*. As if I was making it all up.'

April shrugged. 'Reporters have to have proof.'

Stuart rolled his eyes. The Kingley triplets were always referring to themselves as 'reporters', as if they were writing for some important national newspaper, instead of a flimsy four-page hand-out, invented as a holiday project, printed out in their bedroom and forced on the neighbours.

'I couldn't exactly tell them the truth, could I?' he asked. 'I couldn't tell them that I found a stash of magic threepences, hidden by my great-uncle, together with a note telling me to try and find his lost workshop. I couldn't tell them that I put coins in old slot machines all over Beeton, which ended up leading me to the room under the bandstand. I couldn't tell them that one of the stage illusions I found there was called the Well of Wishes, and it actually *did* grant wishes when you chucked in a coin. They'd think I was mad.'

He couldn't face reading the rest of the article, and instead turned the paper over and looked at the back page.

LADY MAYORESS DISAPPEARS

Jeannie Carr, Mayoress of Beeton (and owner of the Tricks of the Trade Magic Trick Factory and

School of Stage Magic), has not been seen since she went to investigate the room underneath the bandstand. Her assistant, Clifford Capstone (42), claims she was so upset by the damage to the bandstand floor that she decided to resign as mayoress immediately and go on holiday — though he was unable to say where, or for how long.

'Longer than you think,' muttered Stuart. Yet another thing he couldn't tell the other two Kingley sisters was that the 'holiday' mayoress Jeannie Carr had gone on was likely to be permanent, seeing as the Well of Wishes had transported both her and Stuart back to the 1880s, and only Stuart had returned.

'I wonder what Clifford will do now?' asked April idly. 'I know he was desperate to be a magician, but I don't think Jeannie ever taught him anything useful.'

'Just took loads of his money,' said Stuart. 'And kept failing him on Grade Two Basic Magic Skills.'

There was no other news in the paper – only

a list of jumble sales and rubbish collection times. Right at the bottom of the back page was a photograph captioned: *Our ever-ready staff, April, May and June Kingley*. The three clever-looking faces were identical, apart from the fact that April wore glasses.

'Is the photo going to be changed,' he asked her, 'now that you don't write for it any more?'

She shook her head. 'I might stay on. I told June that I didn't want to be the crime reporter any more, but then she said they were looking for an arts correspondent.'

'A what?'

'Someone who'll write about local plays and exhibitions and things. And I thought it might be quite interesting so I've applied for the post. I've got an interview this afternoon.'

Stuart gaped at her. 'An *interview*?'

'Yes. We like to do things professionally. It's at three o'clock, and they'll let me know the result at four.'

Stuart tried not to laugh. In the short time he'd known April she'd proved herself to be clever, resourceful, courageous and loyal, the absolute best sort of friend to have if you were in trouble or in danger. But she was also (he had to admit) a bit of a know-all and one of the bossiest people he'd ever met in his entire life. And her sisters were even worse.

'What are you smirking at?' asked April.

'Nothing.'

She looked at him suspiciously, and then the door opened and Stuart's very tall father came into the kitchen.

'*Salve, o fili*,' he announced, just as the phone in the hall started to ring. He turned back to get it.

'What did your dad just say?' whispered April.

'*Salve, o fili*. It's Latin for "hello, son". You know what he's like.'

April nodded. Stuart's father compiled crosswords for a living, and never used an ordinary, modern word if there was a medieval fourteen-letter alternative.

He reappeared after a few seconds. 'A Mr Felton is desirous of communication with you,' he said.

'Hello,' said Stuart cautiously, taking the phone.

'Rod Felton, Head Curator at Beeton Museum here. You're the youngster who claims to have found the magic tricks, aren't you?'

'Yes,' said Stuart. 'They belonged to my great-uncle.'

'Well, we've had an idea that might interest you. As a matter of fact, it's a job offer. You're still on your summer holidays, aren't you?'

'Yes. For another fortnight.'

'Excellent. If you come to the museum this afternoon, I'll explain . . .'

Chapter 2

'Hello, little chap,' said the museum receptionist, smiling down at him. 'Have you come for the Junior Fun Day story-telling session?'

'No,' said Stuart.

'You get a special hat,' she added encouragingly.

'No,' repeated Stuart between gritted teeth. People were always mistaking him for someone younger; it was one of the worst things about being short.

He continued up the corridor, and then hesitated outside the door of Rod Felton's office.

'What ails?' enquired his father, who had come along too, mainly because the museum had a bookshop.

'Do you think Mr Felton realizes that it was me who broke all that stuff?' asked Stuart.

He was referring to an awful incident that had

happened two weeks before. In a room filled with Victorian farm equipment, Stuart had accidentally nudged a large model of a dairymaid – which had shoved a cart wheel that had toppled a fake blacksmith which had knocked over an enormous artificial horse. The horse had lost an ear and a leg. Stuart's father had written out a large cheque to cover the damage.

'That is something that we shall imminently discover,' said his father cautiously. He reached over Stuart's head and knocked on the door.

'Come in!' called a keen voice. Rod Felton had a great many large teeth, and all of them were on display in a huge smile as Stuart entered the room. 'Aha,' he said. 'The young horse-smasher and his dad.'

'Hello,' said Stuart with a sickly smile.

'Sit down, sit down.' While Stuart and his father squatted on two very low chairs, Rod Felton sat on the edge of his desk and looked down at them.

'Sorry again,' muttered Stuart. 'About the horse, I mean. I honestly didn't—'

Rod Felton held up a hand to stop him. 'We're prepared to forgive and forget,' he said, 'because we in the museum have had what I think is a terrific idea. Our 'Beeton in Wartime' exhibition has come to an end, and we have a two-week gap before 'Roman Beeton' opens, which is obviously going to be a huge crowd-pleasing mega-blockbuster. There's going to be a half-size model of a *triclinium* and a working *balneum*.'

'Would that be a *triclinium stratum*?' asked Stuart's father.

Rod Felton nodded so fast that his head was a blur. 'It would indeed. The *triclinia lecti* are adapted for the *accubatio* and, excitingly, we also have a replica *cathedra* which was based on an illustration in the . . .'

Stuart sat like a lump of wood as the conversation whizzed over his head, most of it in Latin. After a minute or two he held up his hand, as if he were in class. After another minute or two Rod Felton noticed.

'Yes?' he asked.

'You were saying about the terrific idea. To do with my great-uncle's workshop . . .'

'Oh yes, so I was. Well, you know that the

museum offered to store the tricks until a more permanent home could be found for them.'

Stuart nodded.

'Well, we thought that for the next two weeks, while 'Roman Beeton' is being set up and most of the galleries are closed, we could use a side room of the museum to display your great-uncle's stage illusions – we thought we'd call it 'Teeny-tiny Tony's Temporary Tricks'. And – this is the terrific bit – we had the idea of making you the exhibition curator.'

'Me?' asked Stuart incredulously.

'Yes. To demonstrate to other youngsters that the museum is for *everyone*, even people who've behaved badly in the past. You know – *Once I was a vandal and now I'm a helper!*'

'I *wasn't* a vandal,' protested Stuart. 'It was an *accident*.'

'And it would be wonderful publicity,' continued Rod Felton, ignoring the interruption, 'what with you being a relative of Tony Horten. I think we could even get local television to cover it. So would you be interested?'

'What would I have to do?'

'Welcome visitors, tell people about your great-uncle, answer questions about the exhibits and their history. Wasn't there some story about a terrible fire?'

'Yes, Great-Uncle Tony's first magic workshop was in the Horten factory, but it got fire-bombed during the war, and every single illusion in it was totally destroyed, and his fiancée Lily – who was also his assistant – disappeared at the same time. And then Great-Uncle Tony rebuilt his tricks in the secret workshop under the bandstand, before disappearing himself four years later.'

'Excellent,' said the curator approvingly. 'I can see you'd be very good at it. And you'd even have official identification.' He picked up a small object from his desk and held it out to Stuart. It was a badge bearing a cartoon of a toddler wearing a gown and mortarboard, and it read:

I'M NOT JUST A KID
I'M A
MINI EXPERT

'What do you think?' asked Rod Felton.

Stuart hesitated. The badge was awful, the title stupid, and he was pretty certain that any visitors would either ignore him or laugh at him. On the other hand . . .

'Would I be allowed to touch the exhibits?' he asked hesitantly.

Rod Felton looked surprised. 'Of course,' he said. 'As exhibition curator you'd have to know all about the items under your care. Do you want to come and see them now?'

'Yes *please*.'

Stuart started to follow Rod Felton out of the room, and then realized that his father was still sitting on the chair, staring blankly into space – his usual expression when thinking of a crossword clue.

Stuart nudged his arm. 'Dad?'

His father reached into his pocket and took out a tiny notebook and pen. 'Vegetable amidst effort becomes a specialist,' he said dreamily.

'What?'

'The answer's *expert*.'

'Is it?'

'P – as in *vegetable* – in the middle of *exert* – as in *effort*. *Expert*. I'm really pleased with that one. And I've had another exciting thought—'

'Dad, I'm just going to look at Great-Uncle Tony's stuff.'

Mr Horten nodded vaguely. Stuart had long ago realized that his father's definition of 'exciting' was different to most people's. On a scale of 0–10 it would probably look something like this:

0	Visit to a fairground.
1	Free-fall parachute jump.
2	Discovery of an illusion-filled workshop stuffed with magic tricks created by long-lost close family member who mysteriously disappeared fifty years ago.
5	Having a conversation in Latin.
8	Getting a new dictionary for Christmas.
6 trillion	Inventing a crossword clue.

'See you later, then,' said Stuart, following the curator.

'Beeton in Wartime' was being dismantled. An air-raid shelter lay in pieces on the gallery floor, and a dummy wrapped in bandages was leaning against the wall, looking rather sinister.

'Through here,' said Rod Felton, opening a door that had previously been hidden behind a poster about air-raid precautions.

It led into a square, high-ceilinged room, with only a single window near the top of one wall. The curator clicked the light switch a couple of times and then tutted with impatience. 'The bulb must have gone,' he said. 'I'll go and find the caretaker. In the meantime, have a poke around. I'm sure I can trust you not to deliberately damage anything.'

'It was an *accident*,' said Stuart yet again, but the curator had already gone.

Stuart was alone in the room, with his great-uncle's legacy.

Chapter 3

Stuart looked at the cluster of objects draped in dustsheets. When he had discovered Great-Uncle Tony's workshop in the vast and gloomy room under the bandstand in the park, he'd had no time to explore it properly. Beeton Fire Brigade had declared the place unsafe, and Stuart and his companions had been hustled away before he could do more than glimpse most of the contents. Now he stepped forward and pulled at one corner of the nearest sheet.

It slid to the floor, revealing a tall oval cabinet, its surface smooth and ruby red. From the centre of the door protruded the glittering handles of four swords. Stuart reached up and, gripping the lowest, tried to pull the sword out of its slot. It was

17

stuck fast. He let go again and took a step back. There was no lock or handle to the cabinet and no obvious way of opening it. He knocked on it softly, and heard the hollow boom of his knuckles.

'*Enjoy the workshop,*' he said in a whisper. '*It has many surprises.*' Great-Uncle Tony himself had spoken those words to Stuart on the stage of a Victorian theatre, just five days (and a hundred and ten years) ago . . .

There was a noise behind him, and he turned to see Rod Felton coming into the room, holding a stepladder and a light bulb. Close behind him was April.

'I got the job!' she announced gleefully.

'Which job?'

'Reviewer for the *Beech Road Guardian*. And guess what the first thing I'm going to review is?'

'What?'

'This exhibition! Mr Felton's just given me permission to see it – not that there's much to see yet. Shall we take all the rest of the covers off?'

Before Stuart could protest, April had darted past him and was ripping the dustsheets off the other illusions. He felt as if he'd just woken up on Christmas morning and found that someone else was opening his presents. And then Rod Felton fitted the bulb and switched on the light, and the room that had been full of mystery and excitement just a second ago now looked like a brightly lit shop-window display.

'Seven,' said April. 'Seven magic tricks.'

Rod Felton climbed back down the ladder and stood with his hands on his hips. 'What we really need is a name and a short description for each illusion – how it works and so on. Do you think you could make a start on that for us, Stuart?'

'I'll try,' said Stuart.

'Right. I'll leave you to it. Incidentally, er' – he looked rather embarrassed – 'er, your father's still sitting in my office. He seems to be talking to himself. I don't know how to get him out.'

'Tell him the bookshop's about to close,' said Stuart.

The curator nodded and strode out, and the heavy door closed with a bang.

For a moment there was silence.

'So do you know if these tricks even *have* names?' asked April.

'Some of them do,' said Stuart. 'When the mayoress was a little kid, she saw Great-Uncle Tony's stage act – she told me about it.' That had been on the first occasion he'd ever met the mayoress, Jeannie Carr, and he had learned two things about her: the first was that she loved magic tricks, and the second was that she loved money, to a quite frightening degree.

He began to walk around the room. 'The Pharaoh's Pyramid,' he said, lightly touching a golden pyramid, taller than himself.

'The Reappearing Rose Bower' – a bronze throne entwined with silver wire and flowers enamelled in pink and scarlet.

'The Book of Peril' – a giant book, the jet-black cover locked by a huge key.

'The Well—'

'—of Wishes,' finished April, and they both stood for a moment beside the object that had led them on such a manic and magical hunt through Beeton.

'It's odd . . .' said April hesitantly.

'What's odd?'

'The Well of Wishes doesn't look quite the same as it did when it was in the room under the bandstand. I mean, it's the same shape and everything, but . . .'

Stuart frowned. 'It doesn't look any different to me.'

She shook her head. 'I can't put my finger on what's changed, but *something* has. Anyway, what's this one called?' she asked, pointing at a graceful arch made of mirrored glass.

Stuart had no idea, but telling April things she didn't already know was a new and pleasant sensation, so he paused to invent something.

'The Arch of Mirrors,' he said, not very imaginatively. 'And the next one' – he took a moment to consider the giant fan, studded with turquoise jewels – 'is the Fan of Fantasticness, and *this* one,' he said, returning to his starting point, 'is the Cabinet of Blood.'

'Urgh,' said April.

Like Stuart, she tried pulling at one of the

swords, though unlike him she could reach the top one. 'How do you open it?' she asked.

'I don't know yet.'

'Do you see, the base of the cupboard's resting on a sort of disc. I wonder . . .' She gave the sword hilt a sideways push, and the whole cabinet spun round in a blur of red and gold. As the reflections flickered across the room, Stuart noticed something very strange. While the other illusions glinted and flashed in the spinning light, the Well of Wishes seemed to have lost its lustre. No light bounced across its surface. It was as dull as if carved out of rubber.

'You're right about the well,' he said to April.

She nodded slowly, staring in the same direction as him. 'Very peculiar,' she said. 'Anyway, do you want to start the descriptions? I'll take your dictation – I'm a very fast writer.' She whipped her purple reporter's notebook out of her pocket and stood poised.

Stuart felt under pressure. 'I'd better start with the book, I suppose,' he said, 'seeing as I know how it works.' He had climbed into it while hiding from the mayoress in the room under the bandstand.

He walked over to the giant, upright book. The words OPEN AT YOUR PERIL were written across the front in letters of silver and red. He turned the key and lifted the heavy front cover to reveal an empty interior.

April had followed him, still holding the notebook. 'OK,' she said. 'Fire away.'

Stuart cleared his throat. 'When you open the front cover of this illusion, it just looks like a big, empty metal cupboard. But if you get inside it and close the front cover, then the *back* cover opens so that you can climb out the back without anyone seeing you. And then, if someone opens the front cover again, the back cover shuts automatically – so to the audience it just looks like an empty cupboard. And there's a a sort of safety catch at the back which Tony Horten invented.'

He waited for April to stop scribbling. 'Is that all right?' he asked.

'I'll just sub it,' she said. 'That's the phrase us journalists use for improving a story.' She made some rapid notes, and what appeared to be a large number of crossings out.

'OK.' She read from her notebook. '*A disappearing cabinet, in which the front and back covers cannot open simultaneously unless the Horten ready-release mechanism is operated.*' She looked up with a confident smile. 'Next!'

'Hang on,' said Stuart, feeling a bit jangled. 'There's no hurry, is there? This is the first time I've had a chance to really look at everything.'

It was odd to think that no one (apart from himself) had used the trick in nearly fifty years. Great-Uncle Tony's fingerprints were probably still on the inside.

He started to close the cover again, and as he did so, some marks on the floor of the cupboard caught his eye. He crouched down and frowned. Incised into the metal, in very small print, were the words:

AT YOUR PERIL

Chapter 4

'That's odd,' said Stuart. 'It says OPEN AT YOUR PERIL on the front of the book, but down here it just says AT YOUR PERIL.'

April came up and peered over his shoulder at the tiny writing. 'Very odd,' she agreed. 'And why are the words in a box?'

She was right. A rectangle about the size of a pack of cards had been incised around the writing.

There was a pause while they both stared at it.

'You know what?' said April. 'It looks just like a small version of the front cover. Apart from the missing word.'

Stuart nodded. 'Apart from OPEN,' he said softly. There was another pause, and then they spoke simultaneously.

'I know—'

'What if—'

'—the answer!'

'—it's another door?'

They looked at each other, grinning.

'The writing on the front cover's an *instruction*,' said Stuart. 'Open AT YOUR PERIL!'

'Except there's no little key for the mini door,' April pointed out. 'And no handle.'

They squatted down beside the writing. April tried to prise open the tiny door with her fingernails, but it wouldn't shift. 'So how do we do it?' she asked.

Stuart thought about the puzzles that Great-Uncle Tony had set in the past. He thought about the very first puzzle: a tin with a base that unscrewed anticlockwise instead of the more usual clockwise. 'What if it's the opposite of what we expect?' he asked. 'The *front* cover opens if you pull it. So maybe with this one—'

April was there before him. She placed her fingers on the right side of the little door, and gave a push. There was a grating sound, and it sprang upward, revealing a shallow space beneath.

'What's *that*?' she asked.

Stuart reached in and took out a small object wrapped in wrinkled brown paper. It was a six-spoked star made of dark, heavy metal, its surface slightly rippled as if it had melted and then cooled. It was shaped a bit like a miniature cartwheel, but minus the outer rim.

He turned it over on his palm. 'I have no idea . . .' he said slowly. 'A Christmas decoration? Part of a toy?'

'Hang on,' said April. 'Is there something else in there?' She ran her fingers around inside the space and then shook her head. 'No, I'm wrong. There's just a short groove in the bottom.'

Stuart glanced at the crumpled paper that the star had been wrapped in, and with an exclamation began to smooth it out. 'It's a message!' he said, peering at the faded capitals, and April jumped up so that she could read it over his shoulder.

YOU'VE FOUND MY WORKSHOP, BUT DO YOU
WANT TO KEEP IT?

THIS STAR IS MADE FROM ALL THAT WAS LEFT
OF THE FIRST WELL OF WISHES AFTER THE FIRE,
FOR I'VE DISCOVERED THAT ONCE YOU START
USING MAGIC, IT'S VERY HARD TO STOP.

IF YOU TRULY WANT TO BE THE OWNER OF
THESE ILLUSIONS, USE THE STAR TO FIND THE
LETTERS, AND WHEN YOU HAVE ALL SIX, THEY'LL

Stuart turned the note over and April groaned.
There was a wide circular mark on the paper,
almost as if someone had spilled bleach on it. It
blotted out the whole centre of the message:

LEAD YOU TO MY W   OU CAN DECIDE IF YOU
TRULY WISH TO K   RHAPS GIVE THEM
AWAY TO SO   KE CARE AS THE
MAGIC MAY   TTLE STRONGER
THAN I INTE
YOURS AFFE   NCLE TONY

P.S. WHEN I WAS   LOST AN OLD PAL
OF MINE NAMED CH   SO IF YOU SEE
HIM PLEASE LOOK AFT

28

On impulse, Stuart placed the metal star on the page. It was exactly the same size as the missing chunk of writing.

'Strange,' said April thoughtfully. 'But you can still work out what some of the message says. The top bit's about deciding if you really wish to keep the tricks, or whether you want to give them away to someone – but why would you want to give them away?'

'Don't know,' replied Stuart, mystified. 'And what does it mean, "Lead you to my W"? What word's missing there?'

'Winnings?' suggested April. 'Wand? Watch? Wardrobe?'

'And the "old pal" bit. What's *that* about?'

They looked at each other. '"Once you start using magic, it's very hard to stop",' quoted April, her voice breathy. 'It's another puzzle, isn't it? Another adventure?'

Stuart closed his hand over the star, and felt the six prongs dig into his skin. His heart was suddenly thumping; he felt both excited and slightly frightened, and he knew from April's expression that she felt the same. The hunt for Great-Uncle Tony's workshop had been a wild and exciting chase, sprinkled with danger and magic, and now another quest was beckoning. But for what? What was the prize this time?

He felt his hand tingle, and he knew that the object he was holding was so full of magic that over fifty years it had bleached the paper it was wrapped in; he could feel its power.

'I think we should—' he began, and then stopped as the door behind them opened.

'Ah, I have located my offspring,' said Stuart's father, looking pleased. 'I have just been warned by Mr Felton of the impending cessation of visitation hours.'

Stuart groaned in frustration. 'It's closing time,' he translated, for April's benefit.

'He informs me that you may recommence your activities in the morn, the portals being flung wide at nine precisely.'

'So we'll start again tomorrow, then,' whispered Stuart. 'See you here at nine on the dot?'

'Quarter past nine. I've got to deliver the *Beech*

Road Guardian midweek edition first. You won't touch anything till I get here, will you?'

Stuart hesitated. He wanted to start searching for clues this *second*, and the thought of hanging around even for an extra quarter of an hour felt almost unbearable.

'Please,' said April.

Stuart nodded reluctantly. 'OK.'

That evening, Stuart's mother arrived home even later than usual. She was a research doctor in a hospital near Beeton, and most of her days were spent peering through a microscope. Most of her evenings, however, were spent worrying about Stuart (at least, that's what it felt like to him). Unlike his father, she spoke in plain English, and mainly in questions.

'So, do you feel that you're starting to settle down in Beeton?' she asked, sitting on the end of his bed.

Stuart closed his hand over Great-Uncle Tony's message, which he'd been studying. 'Sort of,' he said. He and his parents had only moved to the town four weeks ago, at the beginning of the summer holidays, but it had been four weeks packed with incident, and in some ways he felt as if he'd been living there for years.

'And you've made really good friends with the little girls next door?'

'Sort of,' said Stuart again. He was certainly friends with April, but the other two triplets were another matter.

'And you're not getting too bored?'

'No,' said Stuart, relieved to get an easy question. 'I'm not getting bored at all.'

'Because one of my colleagues is running a junior statistics course for keen young mathematicians next week. I could get you a place on it, if you like.'

'No thank you,' said Stuart quickly. 'I've got tons to do. For a start, I'm curating an exhibition at the museum.'

'Really?' His mother looked astounded. 'I didn't know that.'

'Didn't Dad tell you? But he was there when they asked me. He was sitting right next to me.'

She shook her head, her expression worried.

'Oh well.' Stuart shrugged. 'You know what Dad's like. He was probably trying to think of a long word at the time, and didn't notice.'

His mother smiled, but the worried look remained. 'The thing is,' she said, 'I've just been asked if I can go to a conference in Singapore. It's very last minute – I'd be replacing a colleague who's ill, and I'd be away for nearly ten days. And I'd have to fly out tomorrow afternoon.'

She looked at him anxiously. 'Would that be all right?'

'Of course it would.'

'Can you and Dad manage?'

'Of course we can. I mean, we'll *miss* you, but—'

'Will you eat proper healthy meals and not just pick at whatever's in the fridge?'

'Yes.'

'And change your clothes sometimes?'

'Yes.'

'And go to bed at a reasonable time?'

'Yes.'

'And if you go out during the day, will you stick with friends and leave notes for Dad so he knows where you are?'

'Yes.'

'Because if you only *tell* him things, he forgets. You have to write it down.'

'I know.'

She bit her lip, undecided.

'Don't worry, Mum,' said Stuart. 'We'll be absolutely *fine*.'

Chapter 5

The next morning he got to the museum early and was walking in small, impatient circles outside the main entrance when the caretaker turned up at ten past nine, shortly followed by the curator.

'Don't forget your official identification,' said Rod Felton, and Stuart pinned on his hideous MINI EXPERT badge and then made his way to the side room. Sunlight was streaming through the window.

'Can you finish those descriptions by midday?' asked Rod Felton, popping his head round the door. 'Then we can print them up and laminate them, ready for the exhibition opening tomorrow.'

Stuart nodded, sure that April would remember

a notebook and pen. He checked his watch and frowned. How could she be late when there was so much to do?

He waited another five minutes. Still no April.

He got the little six-spoked wheel out of his pocket and studied it intently from every angle, but there was nothing new to see.

He trudged along to Rod Felton's office and borrowed some scrap paper and a pencil and – as an afterthought – a tape measure.

He wrote THE PHARAOH'S PYRAMID in large careful letters at the top of the page, and then underlined it. Twice. And then checked his watch yet again.

It was ten o'clock.

April was three-quarters of an hour late. She'd said, *Don't touch anything till I get there*, but if he didn't, then he wouldn't be able to describe the tricks properly, and he'd miss Rod Felton's deadline. And besides, they were *his* tricks, even if he couldn't actually prove it to anyone. So of course he could touch them if he wanted to.

'Right then,' he said out loud, secretly feeling

rather pleased. 'I'll just have to start on my own...'

A gold-coloured pyramid, the sides covered
in swirly marks. The base is square, and
each of the four sides is an equilatteral
triangle. The appex of the pyramid is about
1.5m high.

He had to write 'about' because (as usual) he was too short to measure it properly.

Each of the sides has a gold-and-silver
handle right at the top, shaped like a curling
snake. There are no obvios hinges joining the
sides together.

He stood on tiptoe, gripped the nearest snake-shaped handle and pulled. The whole triangular side immediately swung down, cracking him on the head; it was hinged at the bottom, he realized, and was heavier than it looked. He lowered the side to the floor, and stood rubbing his skull for a moment, and then he stooped to get a clearer view of the inside of the pyramid.

It was jet black, so shiny that the varnish still looked wet, and the walls were painted with a scattering of red stars. Stuart took the metal star out of his pocket and held it against one of the painted ones. It was exactly the same size and shape.

He put the star back in his pocket and walked round the pyramid again. However hard he tugged at the handles on the other three sides, none of them would shift.

He lifted the first side up again, and it clicked neatly into position, the pyramid complete once more.

Then he tried one of the other handles again. This time it opened easily.

Grinning, Stuart added a line to his description.

It is only possible to open one side at a time.

He crouched down and stepped inside the pyramid. It was quite roomy – easily big enough for an adult to sit in. He could almost imagine the scene on stage, as Teeny-tiny Tony Horten introduced the trick: '*Ladies and gentlemen, my lovely assistant Lily will now climb into the Pharaoh's Pyramid. As you can see, once the side is closed again, she will have no possible means of escape . . .*'

And yet there had to be a way out: a concealed button, or a spring, or a handle, operated from the inside, so that the assistant could secretly get out. Stuart ran his fingertips over the walls and felt, near the top of each, a little loop of metal, just big enough to hook a finger into and coloured the same jet-black as the rest of the surface. He checked, and found that there was one on the open side as well.

He hooked his finger into the latter and heaved. The side began to swing shut.

Should I wait for April? he wondered.

No, he thought, pulling harder. *I want to solve this myself.*

After all, what was the worst that could happen? He could be stuck inside the pyramid until April or

Rod Felton turned up. A bit embarrassing, but not actually disastrous.

Unless, of course, the pyramid was air-tight.

In which case he might start to suffocate and be found unconscious or possibly dead some hours later, so perhaps it wasn't such a great idea after all – and maybe, on second thoughts, it would be better if he didn't actually fully shut the—

There was a loud and definitive *click*, and Stuart found himself in utter darkness. Not the faintest chink of light was visible. He pushed at the walls but they didn't budge. He pulled at the metal loops: nothing.

'Brilliant,' he muttered, trying not to panic.

And then he saw a glimmer of red light, a glimmer that strengthened and grew and multiplied – a constellation of glimmers all around him. The red stars were luminous!

Nine or ten twinkled from each wall; as he twisted round to look at them, a glimpse of red on the floor caught his eye. One single star shone from the centre of it.

Stuart reached out to touch it, and instead

of a flat, painted surface, his fingers felt a series of grooves and, at the centre of them, a little flat button. Cautiously, he pressed it. There was a metallic squeal, like a hinge in need of oiling, and one of the sides shifted just a little, enough to let in a narrow triangle of light. He gave it a push and it opened completely.

So that's how it worked, thought Stuart. *Great-Uncle Tony's assistant, Lily, would press the button and sneak out of the back, and when Great-Uncle Tony opened up the pyramid for the audience to see, it would be empty!*

It occurred to him that he could play a trick on April to pay her back for being late – he could hide inside the pyramid, wait until she was in the room, and then creep out and surprise her. Confidently this time, he pulled the side shut. He waited for a while in the red-starred darkness before something began to nag at the back of his mind, something about the luminous star on the floor.

Once again he reached down to touch it, and with his fingertips explored the pattern of grooves. There were six of them, radiating out like the spokes of a rimless wheel. He felt a great surge of excitement. He delved into his pocket and took out the metal star – it would fit, he just *knew* it would.

Heart trotting, mouth dry, he slotted the star into place.

The effect was instantaneous.

All four sides of the pyramid fell open with a noise like a thunderclap, and Stuart screamed.

He was in the middle of a desert.

Chapter 6

Slowly, very slowly, Stuart stood up and looked around.

Instead of the side room of Beeton Museum, he saw a sweep of greyish sand peppered with rocks. A few low thorn trees were the only vegetation; not far away, a camel was grazing on one of them. The air was cold, damp and misty, the sky a dirty white. Overhead, a large dark bird was circling.

Stuart shivered. This felt much too real to be a dream.

This was – this had to be – magic.

A breeze ruffled across the plateau, stirring the mist. Stuart waited, still stunned by the sudden change in his world. Where was he? What was he doing here? How could he get back home again?

It's a puzzle, April had said when they found Great-Uncle Tony's letter – but what sort of puzzle was this?

The mist shifted and swirled, like a set of lacy curtains, revealing odd glimpses of a wide and empty landscape. Sand stretched out in all directions. It was so quiet that Stuart could hear the ripping sound of the camel tearing off stringy strips of bark, and then the soft thud of its feet as it moved on to the next tasty branch.

Stuart looked down at his own feet. He was still standing on the square base of the Pharaoh's Pyramid. The six-spoked star lay snugly in its matching slot. The base didn't look broken or damaged, although he noticed that there were two little holes punched in each of the edges.

So where was the rest of the pyramid?

No sooner had the question jumped into his head than a splinter of sun poked through the low cloud, turning the sand from grey to golden. Out of the corner of his eye Stuart saw a bright flash, and turned to see a blinding triangle of light some distance off. Shielding his eyes, he walked towards it and realized that it was one of the pyramid sides, leaning against a huge boulder and reflecting the sun.

At that moment, just behind him, the camel gave a snort and took another step forward. One of its feet made the usual soft thud, and the other a metallic clang. Stuart switched direction and found another of the pyramid sides, this one half buried in the sand. He waited until the camel had moved on, and then heaved the metal triangle out of its resting place. It was heavier than he'd imagined, and one of its edges bore a pair of prongs, sticking out like short, blunt fingers.

'Oh, I get it,' said Stuart out loud. 'I think I get it. It's a *jigsaw* puzzle.'

The third side he found wedged in a rocky cleft, and somebody seemed to have built a camp fire on top of the fourth: it was covered in ash, and a large half-charred log lay across it.

It took him an age to drag the four sides back to the base. The sun was burning off the mist and it was getting hotter all the time; Stuart's T-shirt was dark with sweat. Would it be possible to die of thirst in a magic landscape? There wasn't a scrap of shade to sit in, nothing to drink and nothing to eat apart from a single stick of chewing gum in the pocket of his jeans. He tore it in two and saved one half for later.

Overhead, the large dark bird had been joined by three others. They weaved silently across the deepening blue.

'OK...' murmured Stuart. He braced himself and lifted one of the sides. The two prongs slotted neatly into the two matching holes on the base. Easy!

There was a belch behind him and he turned to see the camel watching with what looked like contempt.

'What?' asked Stuart.

The camel flared its nostrils and went on eating. It was wearing a set of reins, he realized, and the remains of a saddle, having presumably dumped its rider somewhere in the desert.

Stuart turned back to his task.

The second and third sides of the pyramid slotted in just as neatly as the first. Stuart lifted the fourth side, started to manoeuvre it into place, and then paused. He had a sudden horrid vision of the Pharaoh's Pyramid vanishing, leaving him standing alone in the desert. He needed to be *inside* it when it disappeared. He stepped onto the base, crouched down and, with a sense of quiet triumph, slotted the fourth side into place and began to pull it shut.

Immediately, with a dull thud, the other three sides fell over.

Stuart looked round and stared, open-mouthed, at the triangles lying flat on the sand. 'No,' he said out loud. 'Now that's not fair.'

The sun bored into his back. The horizon rippled in the heat.

Stuart got to his feet and gave it a second go. One side, two sides, three sides, four si— And then *wham!* As he pulled the fourth side closed, the other three collapsed back onto the desert floor.

He stood, hands on hips, breathing heavily, panic crawling inside his chest. How was he going to solve this? And what if he *couldn't*? He took a deep breath.

'OK, it's a puzzle,' he said out loud again – somehow it was easier to think in a calm and logical way if he imagined he was talking to someone else. 'And it's *not* just a jigsaw puzzle.'

Grimly, for the third time, he lifted three sides into place. He remembered that there was a small loop right at the top of each, and this time he hooked the fingers of one hand through them. Could he hold up three of the sides while he lifted the fourth?

He reached out vainly.

No, he couldn't, it was too far away – he'd need an arm the length of an orang-utan's.

'If I had a thin rope of some kind,' he said, 'I could slip it through the loop on the fourth side, and pull it up while I was still holding onto the others. But where can I find a thin rope?'

The answer to his question walked by just a few metres away, reins dangling.

'OK,' said Stuart to himself. 'So all I have to do is catch a camel.'

Chapter 7

Stuart had once watched a programme on camels in which it had been shown that they could spit accurately and kick in any direction. But was this camel real, or was it a sort of figment of Great-Uncle Tony's imagination?

He moved closer.

It looked real. It *smelled* real.

'Stay,' he said feebly, edging towards it. 'Nice camel.'

It glanced at him, and then went on ripping at the thorn tree with teeth the size of piano keys. The reins were tied to a woven nose band which fastened just under its chin. Just under its chin and very close to its teeth.

'Good boy.' Stuart remembered the half-stick of

chewing gum in his pocket. He took it out and held
it at arm's length.

The camel stopped eating.

'Here, boy,' said Stuart, his voice sounding reedy
and nervous. 'Yum yum.'

The camel took a pace forward.

'Lovely chewing gum.'

With incredible swiftness, the camel lunged
towards Stuart and snatched the gum out of his
hand. Stuart made a grab for the reins. The camel
tossed its head and Stuart found himself flying
through the air.

'Ow,' he said, landing in the sand several metres
away. The camel gave him a contemptuous look and
then cantered off into the shimmering distance,
chewing as it went. Stuart was left alone.

As he got to his feet, he thought of a phrase in
Great-Uncle Tony's letter:

MAGIC MAY   TTLE STRONGER
THAN I INTE

'A little stronger than I intended,' finished Stuart,

rubbing his leg. And then he noticed something on the ground and stooped to pick it up. It was a length of bark, revoltingly saturated with camel spit, but quite long and stringy nonetheless. He hunted around for some other pieces, and knotted three or four lengths together until they were long enough to thread through the loop. Feeling a bit like a survival expert on the telly, he gave the bark string an experimental tug. It broke. Clearly it needed to be thicker.

'Perhaps if I make three strings and then plait them . . .' he said doubtfully. He'd never done any plaiting, but it couldn't be that hard, could it?

After about three minutes of hopeless twiddling and twisting and unravelling, he caught himself wishing that April was with him. He had no doubt that *she'd* know how to plait – it was just the sort of thing that girls always knew. They'd be out of here in two minutes.

A drop of sweat trickled into his eyes, and he paused to wipe his forehead. His T-shirt was damp, his jeans sticking to his legs, the buckle of his belt so hot that it was actually—

'*Belt!*' shouted Stuart, leaping to his feet. 'My *belt!*'

It took him about six seconds to get back into the pyramid, take his belt off, slip it through the loop on the fourth triangle and grab the loops on the other three sides. He took one last look at the blistering landscape, the circling birds, the blurred and distant blob that was the camel, and then he gave the belt a pull.

As the fourth side closed, the blurry distant blob moved closer, and Stuart realized that it wasn't the camel at all, but something much smaller. Something white and brown. And then, before he could see it properly, the fourth side snapped shut.

Slowly he released his grip on the loops. For a moment all was darkness, apart from the glimmer of red stars, and then Stuart yelled as a vivid green shape writhed suddenly across the inside of the pyramid. It was an emerald S, which stretched and tautened and glowed and grew – and then disappeared utterly as one side of the pyramid opened.

'Are you all right?' asked one of April's sisters, peering anxiously in on him. Behind her, the museum looked reassuringly normal. 'I heard you shouting,' continued May (or June).

'I'm fine,' said Stuart, climbing out, though actually he felt shaky and strange and in dire need of a sofa and a glass of water. 'What are you doing here? Why didn't April come?' he added.

The triplet frowned. '*I'm* April,' she said.

'No you're not.'

'What do you mean *No you're not*? I should know who I am, shouldn't I? *I'm* April and you promised to wait until I got here before you started exploring.'

'But you're not wearing glasses,' said Stuart. 'And you've got a camera.'

She rolled her eyes and sighed dramatically. 'I was on my bike delivering papers, and then I swerved to avoid a hedgehog, fell off and scraped my knee and broke my specs,' she said. 'That's why I got here two hours late. And then I happened to borrow May's camera because I thought it would be useful.'

'Oh.'

'I so wish you'd just *try* to—' she began, and then tilted her head, puzzled. 'Why are your shoes all covered in sand?' she asked. 'And why are your trousers falling down?'

There was a pause in the conversation while Stuart scuttled back to get his belt.

'The thing is,' he said, bending to pick a thorn out of one of his socks, 'you'll never believe where I've been for the whole of those two hours. I don't believe it myself.'

April lost her cross expression and looked at him eagerly. '*Magic?*' she whispered.

'Yes. Definitely.' And he told her about his jigsaw puzzle in the desert. And about the emerald letter S that had greeted his return.

'*Use the star to find the letters!*' exclaimed April. 'That's what the message said, didn't it? Oh, I *wish* I'd come.'

'So do I,' replied Stuart honestly, 'and next time you will.'

'Promise?'

'I promise.' Stuart held out his hand, and April started to shake it and then froze, gazing open-mouthed past his head.

'Look,' she said. 'It's not shining any more.'

Stuart turned. The sun was pouring in through the window, but the golden surface of the Pharaoh's Pyramid barely glinted. It was still a beautiful object, but like the Well of Wishes it had lost its lustre.

'The magic's all used up,' said Stuart wonderingly. 'It's like a flat battery – there's no more power in it.'

Then he remembered the six-pointed star, and ducked back into the pyramid to retrieve it.

'Whatever's the matter?' asked April as he blinked at the object in his hand.

Stuart held up the star so she could see it. One of the six spokes had completely disappeared.

She stared for a moment, open-mouthed. 'So what happens if you put it back in the socket again?'

Stuart tried it. 'Nothing,' he said, taking the star out for a second time. 'So that must mean you can only do each adventure once.'

April nodded. 'One down,' she said softly. 'Five to go.'

Chapter 8

The opening of the exhibition was a bit low-key; only a few people bothered to follow the hand-made sign in the foyer, and most of them were related to either Stuart or April. Inside the room, the only note of celebration was a table with some feeble refreshments.

'Good thing I'm not hungry,' whispered April, grimacing at the plate of plain biscuits and single bowl of crisps before returning to where her parents were looking at the Cabinet of Blood.

Stuart sipped from his cup of watery squash, and watched the guests amble between the exhibits.

Stuart's father was being escorted round by Rod Felton, and although the two men *appeared* to be looking at the Arch of Mirrors, Stuart could hear scraps of Latin floating across the room, and the curator seemed to be miming a Roman sword fight.

April returned to the table and took three biscuits and a huge handful of crisps.

'I thought you said you weren't hungry,' said Stuart. She glowered at him.

'Oh,' said Stuart. 'You're not April, are you?'

'No.'

'June?'

'I'm *May*!' she screeched indignantly. 'Are you *blind*?'

She stalked off towards her sisters and began a whispered conversation with them. Dark looks were cast at Stuart.

He turned away and ate a crisp or two. He couldn't help getting the triplets mixed up – they had the same faces, the same hair and they wore the same sort of clothes. Other than April's glasses there wasn't a single way of telling them apart, yet they went mad if you pointed that out. If they really wanted people to know who was who, he thought, then they should dress in different colours.

'Excuse me?' A soft-voiced man was peering down at Stuart. 'I see from your badge that you're the curator. Though you seem kind of young for that.'

'I'm ten,' said Stuart.

'OK. Well, I'd like to be shown around the exhibition. Is that at all possible?'

Stuart nodded. 'Are you American?' he asked.

'Canadian. Maxwell Lacey – good to meet you.' They shook hands. Maxwell Lacey was wearing an expensive-looking jacket and emerald cufflinks. He looked about the same age as Stuart's father, but had a large black moustache and neatly brushed pale grey hair. 'So how did you get to be in charge?' he asked Stuart.

'Partly because I found the tricks in the first place, and partly because Teeny-tiny Tony Horten was my great-uncle.'

'Really? Well, isn't that something!'

Maxwell Lacey paused by the first exhibit. He leaned over the rope and gazed at the great bronze throne surrounded by intricately worked flowers and tendrils, and then switched his attention to the little card pinned to the wall next to it.

THE REAPPEARING ROSE BOWER

A large bronze seat surrounded by metal stems and flowers. The illusion involves the disappearance and reappearance of the Roses.

'We didn't have a lot of time to write the cards,' said Stuart apologetically, 'and we still haven't worked out how the trick operates, so the second sentence is a bit of a guess. We're going to have another go tomorrow.'

'And by "we", you mean . . .'

'Me and April. One of the triplets over there.'

'And is April also related to Tony Horten?'

'No, that's just me.'

'I see.'

They moved on to the Arch of Mirrors. 'We didn't have a lot of time to look at this one, either,' said Stuart quickly.

THE ARCH OF MIRRORS

An arch that is completely covered in mirrors. How the illusion operates is currently not known.

'It's a fine-looking object,' said Maxwell Lacey, adjusting his tie in one of the many reflections that bounced back at him. 'And this workshop where you found the illusions – was it on your property?'

'No, it was in the town park, underneath the bandstand.'

'I see. And who owns the park?'

'I don't know. The council, maybe?'

As they progressed past the Cabinet of Blood (which Stuart and April still hadn't managed to open) and the Fan of Fantasticness (which they hadn't managed to close), Maxwell Lacey asked several more rather odd questions about local council land ownership.

Stuart was beginning to run out of answers and

was relieved to see one of the triplets approaching him.

'I'm April,' she said pointedly, 'just in case you can't tell. I'm sorry to interrupt, but someone's just turned up who I think you'll want to see.' She squinted over at the doorway.

There, wearing a shiny purple suit with a sparkly bow-tie, and holding a bundle of yellow paper, stood Clifford Capstone. Until a week ago he'd been an unpaid assistant to the mayoress, but had realized her true nastiness just in time and had helped April and Stuart when they'd been in desperate need.

'Hello!' he called, catching sight of them and hurrying over. 'I thought this would be a good place to hand these out. Have a leaflet,' he added, thrusting one into each of their hands.

MYSTERIOSO
THE MAGGICIAN

PERFORMING FOR THE VERY FIRST TIME

HIS

HUGELY EXCITING NEW ACT

'I'm Mysterioso,' explained Clifford, 'just in case you were wondering.'

'You've spelled *magician* wrong,' said April.

'Have I?' Clifford goggled at the leaflet and then looked crestfallen. 'I didn't notice; I've printed out six hundred now – I can't really change them.'

'It doesn't matter,' said Stuart. 'I'll come.'

'And me,' said April. 'And, tell you what, I'll review it for my paper.'

'Will you? I've been rehearsing very hard, but it'll be my first solo show and I'm not convinced I've really come up with the right ingredients yet. Leaflet?' he added, offering one to Maxwell Lacey.

'Thank you kindly,' said the Canadian. 'So this is your hobby, is it?'

Clifford's eager, round face became suddenly

strained and serious. 'It's far more than a hobby,' he said. 'It's what I've always wanted to do. I gave up my job and used up most of my life savings to train as a magician, but now I've realized that the only way to become one is just to go ahead and *do* it.'

'And what type of magic does Mysterioso do?' asked Maxwell Lacey.

'I thought I'd mix and match, seeing as it's my first attempt,' said Clifford. 'A couple of large illusions, a little bit of close-up magic, a wild-animal-based finale. I'll see what goes down best and take it from there. You're interested in magic, I take it?'

'No,' said Maxwell Lacey unexpectedly, 'but my employer is very interested indeed. As a matter of fact, I need to call her now. It's good to meet you people.' Smiling, he folded the leaflet into his pocket and then left the room.

April turned to Clifford again. 'What sort of wild animal are you using in your wild-animal-based finale?' she asked.

'Wait and see,' he said, raising his eyebrows mysteriously. 'I guarantee it'll be a surprise . . .'

Chapter 9

When Stuart came into the kitchen the next morning, he saw two letters pinned to the cork-board. The first was addressed to Stuart's father.

Dear Alan,
Have a lovely time while I'm away. Try and make sure that Stuart eats some vegetables and/or fruit with every meal, and goes to bed before midnight.
Much love to my kind, clever husband, and see you in ten days.
Bernie xxxxxxxxxxxxxxx

The second was addressed to Stuart. As he stood reading it, his father joined him in the kitchen.

Dear Stuart,
Have a lovely time while I'm away.
Be sensible, don't forget to inform
Dad in writing where you are
at all times, and always remember
to take a door-key with you,
just in case Dad goes out and forgets
his.
Much love to my brave, energetic
son, and see you in ten days.
Mum xxxxxxxxxxxxxxx

Father and son looked at each other.

'Orange, banana, peach, plum or melon with your morning repast?' enquired Stuart's father, peering down at him.

'Peach please. And I'm going to the museum all day, with April, and then to St Cuthbert's church hall to see a magic show, with April – I'll write it in a note for you. And I'll take a door-key.'

'And I shall prepare a portable container of noon-tide comestibles for you,' said Stuart's father, going over to the fridge.

'Thanks,' said Stuart. He had a sinking feeling that the contents of his packed lunch were going to be very, very healthy.

April was already waiting for him in the side room of the museum, sitting at the curator's table. He was relieved to see that she was wearing a new pair of glasses. She was also wearing a new badge. 'Rod Felton just gave it to me,' she said, rather gloomily. 'He said it would make me more official. Don't laugh.'

The badge had a picture of a baby in a business suit, sitting at a computer, and it read:

I'M NOT JUST A KID I'M
A REALLY JUNIOR
RESEARCHER!

'You're laughing,' said April.

'No, honestly,' lied Stuart.

'And I've been given a visitor's survey as well,' said April. 'It's got questions like *Do you feel that the exhibition captions give sufficient information?*'

'Well, they don't at the moment,' said Stuart. 'We ought to get started while there are still no visitors to bother us. Do you want to choose which illusion to explore next?'

'OK.' April walked over to an empty space in the middle of the room, closed her eyes, spun round a couple of times and pointed randomly.

'The Arch of Mirrors,' she said, opening her eyes and staggering slightly. 'Two questions: What's the trick of it, and where does the Magic Star fit in?'

'Three questions,' corrected Stuart. 'If we find where the Magic Star fits in, then where will it take us?' *To the desert again?* he wondered. *Or to a different magical world, with a different sort of puzzle?*

He followed April over to the arch. It was nearly as tall as Stuart's father, and every inch of it was covered in mirrors. Each mirror was square and was set at a slightly different angle. In the sunny room, light beams seemed to bounce across the surface like ping-pong balls.

April pushed and then pulled one of the small mirrors. 'It feels quite springy,' she said, 'as if it's supposed to move. I bet one of them lifts up or swings round in some way.'

Stuart walked right round the illusion, seeing his reflection shift and change a hundred times. It would take hours and hours to try every mirror, and it would be easy to lose track and forget which ones had been tried.

'It's making my eyes hurt,' complained April. 'Too many reflections.' She went across to the light switch and turned it off, but sun still flooded in through the single window.

'There's a blind,' said Stuart, going over to where a cord was looped around a hook on the wall. He started to free it.

April had crouched down beside the arch. 'That's odd . . .' she said.

'What?'

'One of them doesn't reflect.'

The blind rattled down, blocking out the sun. Stuart turned round.

The arch had totally disappeared.

'April!' he yelled.

'I'm here!' She was laughing. 'Lift up the blind again.' He hauled it up, and heard himself gasp. The arch was still there, but instead of being covered in mirrors, it was totally black.

'And now look,' said April, still crouching beside it. She fiddled with something, and the mirrors suddenly appeared again, like an eye opening. 'They're all on a swivel,' she explained. 'And one of the mirrors near the bottom isn't a mirror at all, it's just painted to look like a mirror. When you turn it round, they *all* turn round, and the backs of them are coloured black.' She demonstrated again; the arch turned from brilliance to near-invisibility in a second.

'So really,' she went on, 'it's the *Disappearing* Arch of Mirrors. I bet they put the lights down in the theatre, did a drum-roll, and then all the audience screamed their heads off when it suddenly wasn't there any longer. And look here . . .' she added in a quieter voice.

Stuart knelt beside her. On the black side of the painted square was a series of grooves in the shape of a star – a star with just five spokes.

They grinned at each other.

'So maybe that's how it works,' said April. 'We find how the trick operates – the switch or the swivel or the lock or the handle or whatever – and *that's* where the Magic Star goes.' She gave a bounce of excitement. 'So let's get going! This is the next one, isn't it? The next adventure.'

'Yes. Right. OK.' Stuart realized that he was feeling a bit nervous. Those hours in the desert had seemed awfully real, and there'd been times when he'd felt a bit desperate, not to mention hungry and thirsty. He went over to his rucksack and took out a lunch box and water bottle. 'Right,' he said again, steeling himself, half thrilled, half frightened; at least he wouldn't be on his own this time.

He took out the star, and knelt beside the Arch of Mirrors.

'Can we hold hands?' asked April. 'I don't want to be left behind.'

Stuart checked to see that no one else was in the room. 'OK,' he said reluctantly. April grabbed his left hand; with his right, he fitted the five-spoked star into its socket.

And the world went black.

Chapter 10

It was only dark for a second, but when the lights came back on, everything had changed. Stuart was still standing in front of the Arch of Mirrors, but it was smaller than before – no taller than himself – and it was brilliantly lit, as if by a spotlight. The only other object in view was an easel, also spot-lit and facing away from the Arch. Everything else was in utter darkness; Stuart couldn't see whether he was in a room, or a hall, or even on a stage. The silence was total. April was nowhere to be seen. Feeling anxious, he called her name, but his voice sounded thin and weedy, and it disappeared into the gloom, unanswered.

He stepped round to the front of the easel. Resting against it was an empty picture frame.

It was square and about the width of Stuart's out-stretched hand. He could look straight through it and see the arch, a small image of himself reflected in every mirror. Written across the top of the picture frame were the words:

WHO ARE YOU?

Stuart picked up the frame and turned it over but there was nothing written on the back. As he returned it to the easel, he got the sudden feeling that something was wrong – that he wasn't seeing something that he *should* be seeing. For a second time he picked up the frame, and realized with a chill that there was no answering movement from the reflections: all those rows of Stuarts had remained perfectly still . . .

He walked over to the arch. He could see his own face in each mirror, brightly lit in front of a dark background. He could see the blue of his T-shirt, and the dirty smudge that he appeared to have on his right cheekbone. But when he lifted a hand to his face, no hand appeared in the mirrors. He moved closer. The images in the mirrors weren't painted: they had depth, they were alive, they were breathing, but they weren't *reflections*. It was as if each were a TV screen, showing a continuous programme of himself. The Stuart Channel. But each programme was slightly different – one Stuart was smiling, another was biting his lip as if perplexed, a third seemed to be looking off to the left.

'Weird,' said Stuart. He was still holding the picture frame, and on a sudden impulse he placed it flat against the arch. The mirrors that made up the surface were exactly the right size for the frame.

'So do I have to choose one?' he asked out loud.

He glanced from image to image, wondering what he was supposed to be looking for. Stuart after Stuart grinned, sneezed, stared, blinked and shrugged at him.

And, he reminded himself, there were all the mirrors on the other side of the arch as well – he ought to look at those too. He started to walk round it, and then found that he couldn't: his feet were moving, but he made no progress, as if he were walking on a treadmill or an ice rink. After a couple of minutes of panting effort he gave up; clearly he was supposed to stay where he was.

'OK,' he muttered. 'I'll just have to pick one on this side. They're all me, anyway.'

He reached out randomly towards a Stuart who was yawning hugely. The mirror came away after just a single tug. There was a black gap in the arch where it had been.

What now?

Stuart walked back to the easel, fitted the mirror into the frame, and put the frame back on the little ledge where he'd found it.

And instantly the mirror in the frame disappeared.

Stuart looked at it, startled, and even stuck his hand through the hole, just to make sure. And then he went back to the arch. The black gap had filled up again – he couldn't even tell where he'd taken the mirror from.

'So that was the wrong choice,' he muttered. 'I must have to pick out one in particular—'

'I'm bored,' said a voice behind him.

Stuart spun round and saw –

Himself.

He yelled.

Blue T-shirt, smudge on cheek, jeans, scuffed trainers, hands stuffed in pockets.

'I mean, what do you even *do* here?' asked the other Stuart, ignoring the yell. 'This is the dullest place I've ever, ever been to, and I didn't even bring any money with me, so I can't buy anything, even if I found a shop.' He had a slightly whiny, irritating voice.

Do I really sound like that? thought the real Stuart, still reeling from the shock.

Bored Stuart yawned again. 'I mean, it's dark, there's nothing to see, there's nowhere to go, there isn't even anything to sit on, I can't put on any music, I can't—'

'Shhhh!' said the real Stuart. He could hear another voice somewhere, calling his name. He strained his ears.

'I mean, there's only another two weeks left of the summer holidays,' droned Bored Stuart, 'and if I have to spend it in this place, then—'

'Will you please *be quiet*,' said Stuart. He could hear the other voice again, and this time he was certain that it was April.

'I CAN JUST ABOUT HEAR YOU!' he yelled. 'WHERE ARE YOU?'

A moment passed, and then he heard her distant answer.

'IN FRONT OF THE ARCH. ON THE OTHER SIDE TO YOU, I THINK. HAVE YOU DONE IT YET?'

'DONE WHAT?'

'CHOSEN THE RIGHT MIRROR AND PUT IT IN THE FRAME?'

'NO, I DON'T KNOW HOW TO. WHICH ONE'S THE RIGHT ONE?'

'THE ONE THAT'S YOU.'

'BUT THEY'RE ALL ME.'

'NO THEY'RE NOT.'

'YES THEY ARE.'

'NO THEY'RE *NOT*. IF YOU LOOK CAREFULLY, YOU'LL SEE THAT THEY MIGHT LOOK A LOT LIKE YOU BUT THEY'RE NOT *ACTUALLY YOU*. ALL EXCEPT ONE. IT ONLY

TOOK ME A COUPLE OF MINUTES TO PICK THE RIGHT ONE, BUT THEN, OF COURSE, I'M USED TO SEEING PEOPLE WHO LOOK LIKE ME BUT WHO AREN'T ACTUALLY ME.' She sounded (Stuart thought) a bit smug.

'I'm just so bored,' said Bored Stuart.

'Shhh.'

'I can't remember being as bored as this ever, not even when—'

'Just *SHUT UP*,' snapped Stuart.

'WHAT?'

'I WASN'T SAYING IT TO YOU, APRIL.'

'WHO WERE YOU SAYING IT TO, THEN?'

'SOMEONE WHO LOOKS JUST LIKE ME. BUT WHO ISN'T.'

'I mean,' continued Bored Stuart, 'there isn't even a book or a magazine or anything, so how am I supposed to . . .'

Stuart turned and stared at his almost-twin as he drivelled on about how there was nothing to do. He examined every inch of the boy's face, and tried to compare each feature with what he saw in his own mirror every morning. But the trouble was, he hardly ever looked in his own mirror: four seconds for combing his hair, a quick glimpse of his teeth after brushing, and that was it. The truth was – and the realization made him feel more than a little uneasy – *he didn't really know what he looked like.* And he just happened to be in a place where there wasn't a mirror.

'GOOD LUCK,' he heard April shout faintly. 'THE LIGHTS ARE GOING OUT ON THIS SIDE. I THINK I'M ON MY WAY BACK NOW – ACTUALLY, I CAN HEAR SOMETHING ODD. I CAN HEAR A SORT OF CLICKING SOUND IN THE . . .' Her voice faded away.

'APRIL!' he yelled. 'APRIL?'

But there was no reply. He was completely on his own.

'I am *so* bored.'

Well, nearly on his own.

❦Chapter 11

Stuart peered from one image to the next, frowning, comparing, worrying, while Bored Stuart grumbled on in the background. Mirror after mirror showed a boy with shortish hair, greyish eyes, a roundish face and a few brownish freckles. An ordinary sort of face, with an ordinary array of expressions: puzzled, amused, tired, interested—

'Bored. I don't think I've ever been this bored in my whole entire life.'

'Please,' said Stuart, 'I'm trying to think.'

'There is *nothing* to do in here.'

'You could help me work out which of these images is actually me.'

Bored Stuart glanced at the wall of mirrors and groaned. 'But there are *loads* of them. It'll take *ages*.'

'You're not exactly doing anything else, are you?'

Bored Stuart sighed and wandered over to the arch. 'That one,' he said almost immediately, pointing to a mirror on the bottom row.

'You sure?' asked Stuart. 'Why that one in particular?'

Bored Stuart shrugged. 'I dunno.'

'You're just guessing, aren't you?'

'Yeah.'

Stuart stared at the image; it looked just as much like him as all the others. There was nothing to lose. He pulled the mirror off the arch, fitted it into the empty frame and put the frame on the easel. Instantly the mirror disappeared.

Behind him, there was a grunt. 'How many of these can you do in one minute?' demanded a voice.

Heart sinking, Stuart turned. Another Stuart was doing a series of one-armed press-ups.

'I can't do any of those at all,' said Stuart.

'There's no point in being short *and* unfit,' said the other Stuart, a bit breathlessly.

'I'm not unfit.'

'OK, how about some arm-wrestling?'

'No,' said Stuart.

'Arm-wrestling's really *boring*,' said Bored Stuart.

'Are you saying I'm boring?' demanded Fit Stuart, leaping to his feet.

Stuart put his fingers in his ears and walked over to the arch again. It was hopeless. He couldn't tell one image from another, so he'd just have to get lucky. He started pulling off mirrors until he had a huge stack of them, and then, one by one, he put them in the frame . . .

'Bad idea,' muttered Stuart to himself, a bit later. '*Bad* idea.'

The darkness around the arch was filled with Stuarts. Studious Stuart was reading a history textbook. Jokey Stuart was making farting noises with his armpit while Serious Stuart made a disapproving face. Fit Stuart had organized a hurdles race, using Lazy Stuart, Sleepy Stuart and Bored Stuart as hurdles. Boastful Stuart had told everybody beforehand that he was brilliant at running, and had just now lost rather badly to Silent Stuart, who hadn't said anything at all but had so far won the hurdles, the arm-wrestling, and the prize for the largest number of star-jumps in five minutes. The prize had been a spider in a matchbox, donated by Nature-loving Stuart. Moany Stuart had complained about the amount of noise they were all making.

Stuart slapped another mirror into the frame. It disappeared.

'There are a hundred and thirty-seven mirrors in that arch,' said a voice behind him, 'which is one of my favourite prime numbers.'

'Hello,' said Stuart, not bothering to turn round. 'So you're a Stuart who likes maths, are you?'

'Yes.'

'Then what are the chances of me finding one particular mirror, if every time I choose wrongly, a new one appears?'

'Infinite.'

Stuart nodded dully. 'I thought so,' he said.

Suddenly feeling exhausted, he sat down and put his head in his hands.

'I don't know what to look for,' he muttered. 'What makes me *me*? What am *I* best at? I'm not sporty, or mathematical, or swotty or jokey.'

'Got anything to eat?' asked Greedy Stuart, prising open Stuart's lunch box and then making a face when he saw the healthy contents. 'Is this all you've got?' he said disgustedly. '*Salad?* And *fruit?*'

'It's healthy,' said Stuart.

And he remembered the letters his mum had written – one to his dad all about making sure Stuart was eating healthily (*much love to my kind, clever husband*), and the other to himself (*much love to my brave, energetic son . . .*)

So maybe that's who he was – Energetic, Brave Stuart. But how could he see those things in a mirror? And anyway, just because his mum had said them, didn't make them true – mums were always boasting about their kids, and half the boasts were exaggerated. By 'energetic' his mum only meant that he was keener on *doing* things than *thinking* about them (his school reports always said: *Stuart is an energetic boy*, as if that wasn't a very good thing to be). And by 'brave', she was probably referring to the time when (aged four) he'd apparently dragged a stepladder halfway across the garden to try and rescue a cat which had got stuck up a tree. She was always telling people the story of how the cat had scratched little Stuart, and then he'd fallen off the ladder and landed on his chin, and how if you looked carefully . . .

Stuart sat up straight and slapped a hand to his chin. If you looked carefully, *you could still see a sort of little crease where he'd had two stitches.*

He scrambled to his feet, ran across to the arch and began peering at the mirrors.

'What are you doing?' asked Bored Stuart in a bored voice.

'Looking for a Stuart with a tiny scar like the one I've got on my chin. Can you help?'

'Sounds a bit boring.'

'*I'll* be able to find it,' said Boastful Stuart. 'I'm really, really observant – in fact my teacher says I'm the most observant child she's ever met. She put that in my end-of-term report.'

'Well, get on with it then,' said Stuart, still searching.

'I bet I can find it first,' said Fit Stuart, bouncing on his toes. 'Get ready. Get set. *Go!*'

'What about a "loudest burp" competition instead?' said Jokey Stuart, and then burped incredibly loudly, and raised his arms in triumph. 'I've won!'

Stuart felt a tap on his arm. It was Silent Stuart, and he was pointing at the other end of the arch. Stuart followed him across. Silent Stuart placed a finger on one mirror, and Stuart peered at the image. And there it was – the little indented scar on the chin.

'Thanks,' said Stuart hoarsely.

'You're welcome,' said Silent Stuart.

'So you can speak?'

'Only when I have to.'

'So what are you doing the rest of the time?'

'Thinking.'

'Oh. Perhaps I ought to do a bit more of that.'

Silent Stuart grinned, and together they went back to the easel. Stuart fitted the mirror into the frame, and suddenly the vast dark space full of arguing, moaning, yawning, sprinting, burping Stuarts was empty. Only Stuart himself was left, and the mirror in the frame was now just a mirror. Stuart frowned, smiled and yawned, just to make sure that his reflection did the same, and then he went over to the arch again.

It too had changed. Instead of rows of Stuarts, each mirror now showed the image of an identical letter.

A wide silver W.

The light began to fade slowly, as if someone were turning a dimmer switch. The silver letters dwindled and disappeared. For a second there was complete darkness, and then the light flashed on again, and Stuart was back in the museum, blinking with the shock of it.

'At *last*!' said April, who was sitting on the high bronze throne of the Reappearing Rose Bower, surrounded by the curling stems of a hundred metal flowers. 'You've been ages and ages. And I've been dying to tell you what I've found.'

Chapter 12

'What?' asked Stuart, still a bit dazed. When he'd left, the room had been sunlit, but now the sky through the window was heavy with dark clouds, and the odd drop of rain streaked the glass. 'Just a moment,' he added, going over to the Arch of Mirrors and retrieving the Magic Star from its socket. Before the adventure, it had had five spokes; now only four remained.

April waited for him to return. She looked rather grand, sitting high on the throne, her legs crossed.

'The reason I took ages was because I kept getting the wrong Stuarts,' said Stuart. 'How did you find the right April so quickly?'

She shrugged. 'Easy. Like I said, I just looked for the one that was me. The one with my expression.'

'What expression's that?'

'Sort of decisive and determined. It's what makes me stand out from my sisters.'

'And what expressions have they got?'

'June's very, very serious and May's just mad and hysterical.'

'Is she?'

'You know, once you start observing instead of just *guessing*, you'll find it quite easy to tell us apart,' said April, sounding like a particularly bossy teacher. 'Anyway, I want to explain about what I found. I was sitting here eating my lunch, and I accidentally dropped a grape down the side of the seat. When I tried to reach for it, I felt a funny little lever.'

'What happens when you pull it?' asked Stuart, suddenly curious.

'I didn't try,' said April, looking a bit offended. '*Obviously* I was waiting for you.'

'Well, try it now.'

'OK.'

April slipped her hand down next to the seat and pulled something.

Clickety-clack.

She let out a squeak of surprise as the twining rose stems snapped together into a tight thicket, surrounding the whole throne like a silver basket.

For a moment Stuart couldn't work out whether he was witnessing machinery or magic. 'Are you still in there?' he asked, trying to peer between the branches. He couldn't see a thing.

'Yes, I'm here.' April sounded slightly nervous. 'A sort of silver band has snapped across my middle. A bit like a seat belt.'

'Pull the lever again,' suggested Stuart.

'OK. Here goes.'

Clackety-click.

This time she gave a loud scream.

'April?' called Stuart worriedly.

'*Get me out!*' she yelled. Some good hard kicks came from somewhere inside the illusion.

'Where are you?'

'Hanging *upside down*. The whole throne flipped over.'

'So that's why there's a seat belt,' said Stuart thoughtfully.

'But how do I get out?'

'Pull the lever?'

'OK.'

Clickety-clack.

Instantly the twining rose stems relaxed into their starting position, and Stuart could see the throne again.

It was empty, though, and it looked somehow ... different. There was a pattern on the seat that hadn't been there before.

He ran a hand over it and felt a trio of grooves beneath his fingers – a wheel with just three spokes.

'It's here!' he exclaimed. 'The place where the Magic Star goes. There must be *two* thrones, one on top and one underneath, and they revolve.'

'Can I *remind* you,' shouted April from some-where directly beneath him, 'that I am still hanging *upside down* in *total darkness*.'

'Sorry. Try the lever again.'

Clackety-click.

With a rattle and a screech, the rose stems snapped shut once more, blocking the view of the throne.

'Still *upside down*,' shouted April, by now sounding rather cross.

'Pull it again.'

Clickety-clack.

There was another scream from behind the basket of stems.

'Right way up now,' she called through gritted teeth. 'One more pull.'

Clackety-click.

The bower screeched open to reveal April, looking red-faced, her hair sticking up in dusty clumps. She got out hastily. 'That was *not* nice,' she muttered, brushing herself down.

'But we've found out how the trick works, and where the star goes,' said Stuart encouragingly, trying to cheer her up.

She folded her arms and looked back at the throne. 'Hmm. There's just one problem, though, isn't there?'

'What?'

'Who's going to use it?'

'What do you mean?'

'You can only put the star in the right place

when the lever's been pulled and the seat's flipped over. So only one of us will be able to go on the adventure. The other one will spend the entire time hanging upside down in a fifty-year-old metal box full of dust and *insects*.' Delicately, she picked an earwig off her T-shirt and flicked it away.

'Right,' said Stuart, nodding. 'I get you. In any case, it's not the next adventure, it's the one after next.'

As he spoke, there was a brilliant flash outside, followed by the grumble of thunder. As lightning flooded the room, they both saw that there were three illusions now that failed to sparkle in the sudden brightness – the Well of Wishes, the Pharaoh's Pyramid and the Arch of Mirrors.

'I forgot to say – did you see a letter W,' asked April, 'reflected in the mirrors right at the very end?'

Stuart nodded. 'So we've found an S and a W so far.'

'I wonder . . .' began April thoughtfully.

'What?'

'I wonder what they're leading us to? We still don't know, do we? When you were following the trail of coins, you knew you were searching for your great-uncle's workshop. But one by one, we're squeezing the magic out of these tricks – what's going to be left at the end?'

Before Stuart could think of a reply, his stomach gave a loud growl and he realized how hungry he was. He'd left his lunch box in the roomful of Stuarts and it seemed hours since breakfast. He checked his watch and was startled to see that it was a quarter past five.

'Aren't we supposed to be going somewhere?' he asked, frowning.

April smacked a hand to her mouth. 'Clifford's performance! I totally forgot!'

They ran.

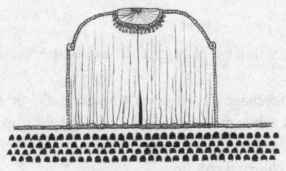

Chapter 13

The entrance to St Cuthbert's church hall was down a dingy alleyway between a pub and a butcher's shop. A board was propped against the wall, with the words: MAGIC SHOW THIS WAY, 6 P.M! handwritten on it, the letters blurred by the brief rain shower. A tiny queue was waiting outside the door. It consisted of a teenage girl, a very small boy and three older ladies.

April got out her notebook and scribbled something.

'What are you doing?' asked Stuart.

'I'm supposed to be writing a review for the *Beech Road Guardian*,' she said. 'I'm just setting the scene.' She showed him what she'd written:

A small but enthusiastic crowd gathered eagerly outside the hall.

'They don't look very enthusiastic to me,' said Stuart.

The teenage girl was checking her make-up in a mirror, while the boy sucked on a huge gobstopper. He kept taking it out of his mouth to check whether it had changed colour.

'Why's it gone all *wed*?' he asked.

'Don't know,' said the girl.

'It was all *gween* and then it went all *wed*. How did it go all *wed*?'

'No idea,' said the girl. 'You'll drop it if you keep doing that,' she added.

'I won't. Why isn't it square? Why's it *wound*?'

'Because it just is.'

One of the old ladies tapped the girl on the shoulder. 'Is that your little brother?' she asked.

'Yes.'

'Aren't you a kind girl taking him out!'

'Mum's paying me,' said the girl. 'She said he was driving her mad with his questions.'

'Why are we waiting here?' asked the boy. 'Why can't we go *in*?'

Just as he spoke, the door opened to reveal

Clifford, dressed in a badly fitting silver suit and with a large sticking plaster on one hand.

'Sorry to start so late,' he said, 'but I had a bit of a problem with the wild-animal finale. Come on in.'

They filed into the hall. About a hundred chairs were arranged in rows, and a purple curtain drooped in front of the stage. Clifford disappeared behind it, and Stuart and April sat down in the front row. April did some more scribbling.

A late start was due to the magician being savaged by a wild beast.

'You make it sound as if his arm was hanging off,' said Stuart.

'Reviews have to be *dramatic*,' replied April loftily, 'otherwise no one will read them.'

From behind the curtain came a short burst of spooky music, and then all the lights went out, apart from a flickering green EXIT sign above the door.

'Oooh,' said one of the old ladies. 'Exciting!'

There was a long pause before the curtains opened in a series of jerks, revealing a darkened stage. After a moment a desk lamp clicked on, and Clifford hurried into the feeble spotlight, pushing a small trolley decorated with silver stars.

'Welcome,' he said, 'to the marvellously mysterious world of Mysterioso the Magician. A world where anything can happen – where red handkerchiefs can turn green . . .'

He took a red handkerchief out of his pocket, stuffed it carefully into one fist, said, 'Abracadabra,' and pulled it back out again.

'It's gone *gween*!' said the small boy in an awed voice. There was a smattering of applause.

'A world where green handkerchiefs can turn red . . .' continued Clifford, doing the same trick again, only in reverse.

'And now it's gone back to *wed*,' said the small boy, slightly less awed.

'Yes, a mysterious and magical world where a blue handkerchief can turn yellow . . .' announced Clifford, taking a blue handkerchief out of his pocket, and doing the whole trick all over again. 'And where a yellow handkerchief can turn blue!'

This time, only Stuart and April applauded.

'I'm getting a bit tired of handkerchiefs,' whispered one of the old ladies rather loudly.

Clifford grinned bravely. 'A mysterious and magical world, ladies and gentlemen, where a white handkerchief can turn . . .'

There was a wail from the small boy, and the noise of something small and round rolling across the floor.

'I've *dwopped* it!'

'I told you you'd drop it,' said his sister irritably.

'I've dwopped my sweet!'

'Oh, the poor little chap's dropped his gob-stopper,' said one of the old ladies sympathetically. 'Pam, have you got a toffee in your bag?'

'Yes, I think I have. Hang on a moment.'

'And a *black* handkerchief can turn *white*!' shouted Clifford, trying to drown out the noise of wailing and rustling.

'Bleach,' said the old lady called Pam. 'That's how I turn my black handkerchiefs white. Or you can wash them in vinegar and leave them out in the sun.'

'I use tissues,' remarked her friend. 'More hygienic.'

Clifford used the white handkerchief to mop the sweat from his forehead. 'And now,' he said, 'I just need a couple of moments to prepare my next trick.'

It was while Clifford was rummaging around at the side of the stage that Stuart heard a tentative knock on the outside door. There was a pause, and then a second knock, and since Stuart was nearest to the end of the row, he walked across to open it.

It was a small pale woman in overalls, a large canvas bag slung over one shoulder, a coil of cable over the other. 'The hall caretaker called me about an electrical problem,' she said. 'Something about an exit sign that keeps going on and off.'

Stuart nodded, and pointed up at the flickering sign above the door. 'It's there,' he whispered, 'but there's a show going on at the moment.'

'OK. Can I wait at the back till it's finished?'

'I suppose so.'

On the stage, Clifford clumped back into view. 'Sorry to keep you,' he said, 'but I hope you'll find it was worth the wait.'

The next bit of the act was a card trick, during

which Clifford dropped the entire pack on the stage and had to spend about a minute and a half crawling around picking them all up again. After that, he sawed a teddy bear in half and then placed a small pot plant into a disappearing cabinet.

'And now we spin it round three times,' he announced, 'open the door and—'

'It's still there!' yelled the small boy. '*Why's* it still there?'

Clifford slammed the cabinet door again, and gave a desperate smile. 'There's just time for the exciting animal finale,' he announced. 'I'll take a moment to set it up.'

He clumped off-stage again.

April nudged Stuart. 'What do you think?'

Wordlessly he shook his head.

Clifford reappeared carrying a large empty cage which he lowered, with an effort, onto the floor at the centre of the stage.

'This cage,' he announced, 'is secure in every way. Do not be afraid, ladies and gentlemen, that the wild beast inside will escape and cause havoc and mayhem in the audience.'

'But there's *nuffing* inside!' piped up the small boy indignantly.

Clifford actually looked quite pleased at the interruption. 'Aha!' he said. 'There's nothing inside at the moment, but I shall drape this magical and mysterious cloak across the cage' – he hung a silver cape over the front – 'and say the magic word, and then you may discover that it's not quite as empty as you think . . .'

For the first time, an air of tension gripped the audience.

'I fink it's going to be a cheetah,' whispered the boy, 'or a buffalo, or a great big, huge, giant, horrible *snake*.'

'I, er . . . don't like snakes much,' said April, sounding uncharacteristically nervous.

Clifford stepped forward. He rapped the top of the cage solemnly three times, shouted, 'Abracadabra!' in a slow, booming voice, and then whipped the silver cape away again and stood triumphant.

The occupant of the cage gave a slight snuffle.

Without taking her eyes away from it, April nudged Stuart. 'Am I going mad,' she whispered, 'or is that a *hedgehog*?'

Chapter 14

'Yup,' replied Stuart. 'That's a hedgehog, all right.'

The hedgehog gave a sneeze, trotted straight between the bars of the cage and rolled up into a ball near Clifford's foot. Clifford bowed and the faded purple curtains swung shut. Only Stuart and April clapped; the rest of the audience left rather quickly, everyone (apart from the small boy) hurrying past a money box labelled:

IF YOU ENJOYED MYSTERIOSO THE MAGICIAN'S ACT FEEL FREE TO SHOW YOUR APPRECIATION!

'Come *on*!' called the boy's sister. He dropped something into the money box and ran out after her.

Stuart glanced at April, who was sitting with the notebook and pencil on her lap. 'What on earth are you going to write in the review?' he asked.

'I have no idea,' she said slowly. 'That was the worst act I've ever seen in my entire life, and that includes watching my dad come last in a karaoke competition at my school in front of me and all my friends.'

A door opened at the side of the stage, and Clifford came through, still dressed in his silver suit. He waved at them nervously. 'Well?' he asked. 'What do you think?'

Stuart opened and shut his mouth a couple of times, but no sound came out.

'Interesting,' said April in an unconvincing squeak. 'Unusual.'

'I was completely stumped for a finale until I found that little fellow crouched by the side of the road the other day, and I thought, *I've never seen a hedgehog in a magic act – I wonder why no one else has ever thought of it*? Brilliant idea, wasn't it?'

'Mmm,' said Stuart, nodding vigorously.

'So, is there anything I should change for the next performance?' asked Clifford.

'The *next* one?' echoed Stuart.

'I've booked the hall again for Thursday – I need the experience. I'm serious, you see – being a magician is all I've ever wanted to do. I have to keep *trying.*'

'Right.'

'So should I change anything, do you think? The order of the tricks? The costume? The music?'

While Stuart was still working out what to say, an answer came in a small shy voice from the other side of the hall.

'The lighting.'

It was the electrician. She was kneeling beside the door, a pair of wire-cutters in one hand.

'Why? Wasn't it bright enough?' asked Clifford.

'Too bright,' she said. 'Much too bright.'

'But don't you want to see what's going on?'

'Not if it's awf—' She bit her lip. 'I mean ... I didn't mean ...'

There was a horrible silence.

Clifford went rather pale, and then turned back

to Stuart and April. 'Was it awful?' he asked quietly. 'Please tell me the truth this time.'

They looked at each other, and then back at Clifford.

'Yes,' they said.

'Really awful?'

'Yes.'

'Even the hedgehog?'

There was a pause.

'*Especially* the hedgehog,' said April. 'The audience was hoping to see a gorilla or something, so it was a bit of a disappointment. Sorry.'

Clifford nodded sadly. He walked over to the money box by the exit, flipped open the lid, took out a dusty, half-sucked gobstopper and stared at it for a while. 'Yes,' he murmured. 'It's true. I was awful,' and then he turned to the electrician, who was still kneeling by her bag. 'Thank you for being honest when nobody else was,' he said. 'I see now that I'm just fooling myself. Jeannie was wrong about most things, but she was right to keep failing me on Grade Two Basic Magic Skills. I'll go back to selling carpets – I was quite good at that.'

'No!' The electrician stood up, her face scarlet. 'I didn't say it to be horrible. I meant it about the lighting – there was no mystery. You can do wonderful things with lights. You can change everything – turn the ordinary into the extraordinary, the awful into the amazing. I'll show you . . .' She fumbled in her bag and took out a long, heavy torch. 'Now watch.'

She went through the door by the stage, and pulled open the curtains. Then she started fiddling in a metal box by the side wall. After a moment there was a click and a thud, and the hall was plunged into total darkness. A few seconds later, there was another, softer click. A beam of light shot upward and a vast shadow appeared on the back wall of the stage. Stuart gasped and stepped back. The monstrous silhouette curled and writhed, a creature from a nightmare, its head crowned like a deadly halo with vicious spikes.

The monstrous, terrifying silhouette opened its enormous, sabre-toothed, bloodthirsty mouth and gave a tiny sneeze.

The lights went back on, and there was the

electrician carefully cradling the very small hedgehog.

'*Wonderful!*' shouted Clifford, awestruck.

'Just very basic lighting,' said the electrician, blushing slightly.

'*Incredible!*'

'Easy.'

'*Amazing!*'

'It's honestly quite straightforward.'

'What we need to do is have a *talk*,' said Clifford eagerly. He sprinted over to the stage, and within seconds he and the electrician were deep in conversation.

'Let's go,' said Stuart to April. He fished a 10p out of his pocket, and dropped it in the box as they left.

By the time they arrived at Beech Road, his stomach had started making loud squelching noises. 'Sorry,' he said to April, 'but I haven't eaten anything since breakfast and it must be nearly half past seven now. I really hope Dad's made pizza. Or spaghetti. Or chips.'

He opened the door and smelled beetroot.

'Hi, Dad,' he said, entering the kitchen. There were pots and pans everywhere, the sink was crammed with washing-up, and cookery books lay piled beside the stove. 'What's going on?'

'A domestic culinary extravaganza,' said his father, whose glasses had steamed up in the heat, 'in keeping with your mother's exhortation to keep you supplied with sufficiently nutritional comestibles.'

Stuart looked around and saw a mountain of peelings. Depression swept over him. He suddenly missed his mum. 'You mean you're cooking hundreds of vegetables?' he asked.

His father nodded. 'Beetroot consommé, followed by leek, carrot and broccoli gratin accompanied by a salad frisée of endive, curly kale, mange-tout peas and bacon.'

'Bacon?' repeated Stuart keenly.

'Actually,' admitted his father, 'I recall that I was so absorbed in the preparation of the vegetable content of the salad that I omitted to add the bacon.'

'You mean you forgot to put bacon in the bacon salad?'

'A regrettable error.'

'So it's a vegetable starter, followed by a vegetable main course with a side helping of vegetables? And none of the vegetables are potatoes?'

'Indeed.'

Stuart groaned but he actually felt like stamping his feet, or even lying down on the floor and having a huge roll-around tantrum like a toddler. 'I want a *burger*,' he muttered under his breath. 'A triple cheeseburger with a double helping of *fries*.'

His father had already started ladling out purple soup. 'And how was the exposition of prestidigitation?' he asked over his shoulder.

'I don't know what you're talking about,' said Stuart crossly.

'The exponent of legerdemain?'

'Nope. Still don't understand.'

'The magic show?'

'*See*,' said Stuart rudely. 'You don't *have* to talk in long words all the time – you can speak just like other people when you try, can't you?' And then, ignoring the hurt look on his father's face, he grabbed a family packet of crisps from the cupboard, and ran all the way up to his bedroom.

He sat and ate them without much enjoyment, knowing that he'd been rotten. Downstairs, the phone rang. He heard his father answer it, and then he heard footsteps coming up the stairs, followed by a gentle knock on his door.

Stuart opened it.

'It's for you,' said his father, holding out the phone.

Chapter 15

Stuart took the receiver.

'Hello?' he said.

'*The kid?*' asked a crackly American voice, the voice of someone extremely old. '*Are you the kid?*'

'Which kid?' asked Stuart. His father was already heading downstairs again, his shoulders drooping rather sadly.

'*The kid who found the tricks?*'

'Yes. My name's Stuart.'

'*Well, thank my stars I can understand you. The guy who answered the phone – was he speaking in code, or what? I never heard a bunch of words like that in my whole life.*'

'That's my father,' said Stuart. 'He's very clever,' he added loyally.

'*And how about you? Are you clever? Or are you smart – which is a whole heap better than being clever?*'

'Excuse me, but who *are* you?' asked Stuart.

'*You can call me Miss Edie. Maxwell Lacey told me he thought you were a smart boy.*'

'Who's Maxwell Lacey?'

'*He's a lawyer. Works for me. He came to see your tricks in the museum – grey-haired fellow with a moustache.*'

'I remember. He kept asking me if I was related to Tony Horten, and whether the tricks had been found on council property. He went on and on about it.'

'*Lawyers aren't paid to be interesting.*'

'But why did he want to know?'

'*Because I'd given him a job to do.*'

'What job?'

'*To buy the tricks. Buy them all. And if he's going to buy them, he needs to find out who owns them.*'

'I do,' said Stuart.

'*Can you prove that?*'

There was a pause, and then Stuart shook his

head, forgetting for a moment that he was on the phone. The voice on the other end of the line was so vivid and vital that he could almost picture the speaker: ancient and white-haired, but crackling with life.

'*Well?*' she demanded, still waiting for her answer.

'No . . .' he said hesitantly. 'I can't prove it.'

'*I thought so.*' She gave a dry laugh that ended in a cough. '*And I spoke to Maxwell Lacey earlier today. He's been poking about in the basement of that town library of yours and he's found a local law that says everything found on council property belongs to the mayor, unless there's legal proof otherwise. And where's your mayor?*'

'She disappeared,' said Stuart.

'*I know she did. So there's a mess. You've got no proof, and the town's got no mayor. Could take years to sort out. And I don't have years – I might not even have months – and I want those tricks.*'

'Why?'

'*I promised my gramma I'd get them.*'

'Your grandma? But she must be . . . I mean,

the tricks are about fifty years old, and surely your grandma must have—'

'*My gramma died eighty-five years ago.*'

'But—'

'*And before she died she told me something I've never forgotten. Hidden in one of the tricks – it's well hidden, she said – is Tony Horten's will. And it leaves everything to the person who finds it.*'

'But—'

'*It'd be all the proof you'd need. Find that will and the tricks are yours to keep.*'

'But—'

'*Or yours to sell. I'd pay you a good price for them.*'

'Hang on,' said Stuart. He felt as if he were being buffeted by a strong wind – strong enough to push him in a direction that he didn't want to go. He tried to make his voice sound firm and certain. 'Hang *on*. Even if there *is* a will – and I still don't understand how your grandma could possibly have known that – and even if I could find it, I don't want to sell the tricks. If I can actually prove they're mine, then I want to keep them.'

'*Fine words.*'

'But I really mean it.'

'*I see.*' The speaker coughed again – a dry, jagged sound. '*You know, there's something particular about me that you don't know,*' she said.

'What?'

'*I'm rich. Very, very rich. I am Rich with a great big golden capital R. My gramma was a businesswoman, the smartest you could ever meet. She left England with ten pounds in her pocket and a headful of ideas, and she set up a factory here in Canada and made more money than you would ever believe. It's all mine now. I'm the last one left, and I can give away as much of it as I like. Do you know what it means to be rich?*'

'No,' said Stuart.

'*It means you can get anything you want. What do you want, Stuart?*'

Stuart hesitated. 'Nothing that I can buy,' he said.

'*Now that's an interesting kind of answer. Let me see if I can guess what you mean . . . Maxwell Lacey tells me that you're new in town and you're just a little fella – smaller than the other kids. Must be hard, especially when you're starting at a new school in a couple of weeks' time. Kids can be cruel, especially kids you haven't grown up with, and if you've got a name like S. Horten, then you're going to get a nickname real quick. Am I right?'*

Stuart said nothing but he could feel his face grow hot. He thought of all the times in his life he'd been called Shorty Shorten. The phone was sticky in his grasp. Miss Edie's voice continued, crackly and compelling.

'Money sure can't buy you height but it can buy you power. The best bike in town, the best computer, the best sneakers, the best parties, the best holidays – you ever been to Disneyland?'

'No,' muttered Stuart, his voice hoarse.

'You could take the whole class. Wouldn't matter how tall you are then, they'd respect the hell out of you. Take the whole class, except anyone who's mean to you. Buy a Rolls-Royce and a chauffeur to carry you to school, and only give lifts to the kids you like. Buy a house with a swimming pool in the back garden, and see how nice everyone is to you then. Friendship's like any other commodity, Stuart

– you can buy it if you have enough money . . .'

Stuart's chest was thudding as if someone inside it were banging a drum.

'You still there?' asked Miss Edie.

'Yes.'

'You have a real think about what I said. Find that will and I can make your dreams come true. They won't call you the shortest kid in class any more – they'll call you the richest . . .'

'But—'

Before Stuart could say any more, the line went dead.

Chapter 16

He stood staring at the silent receiver, and then something tugged insistently at the back of his mind, and he fetched the tin money box in which he kept his most treasured possessions, and took out Great-Uncle Tony's note.

USE THE STAR TO FIND THE LETTERS.
WHEN YOU'VE FOUND ALL SIX, THEY'LL
LEAD YOU TO MY W

'Lead you to my will,' said Stuart quietly.

So that was it, then – the letters were clues that would lead him to his great-uncle's will, and when he found it, he would have a choice.

For a strange moment he felt as if he were

standing on a bridge over a dark, rushing river. On one side of the bridge was a feast of magic: Great-Uncle Tony's illusions, and the bizarre adventures that Stuart and April were finding within them. On the other side was a world of money, glittering with all the things that Stuart could buy, if only he were rich. He stood poised in the centre of the bridge, like an iron filing between two magnets.

And then his father called his name from downstairs and he found himself back in the real world, ravenously hungry, and a bit ashamed of himself.

'Sorry, Dad,' he mumbled, coming into the kitchen. 'Sorry I was rude to you.'

'Expiation delightedly accepted. I surmise that you were sorely in need of sustenance and therefore I have prepared a porcine-based comestible.'

He waved a hand towards the table, and Stuart looked at the large, delicious-looking sandwich, stuffed with bacon and oozing tomato sauce. And then he looked at all the other things that his father had spent the entire afternoon cooking.

'Can I have some soup as well?' he asked. 'And maybe a small slice of the vegetable flan and a bit of salad. Just a small bit?'

After five minutes of steady chomping, Stuart felt much fuller and much, much healthier.

'Thanks, Dad.'

His father was looking thoughtful. 'Do you think it might aid mutual colloquy if I endeavoured to converse in a less polysyllabic manner?' he asked.

'What does *mutual colloquy* mean?'

'Our conversation.'

'And *endeavour* means *try*, doesn't it?'

'Indubitably.'

'So what you're saying is, *Would it be easier for us to talk if you used shorter words?*'

'Yes.'

Stuart nodded cautiously. 'Well, it might speed things up a bit. What do you want to talk about?'

'I confess to a mild sense of curiosity about your recently completed telephonic communi—' His father paused and swallowed. 'Your phone call,' he said, rather slowly, as if speaking a foreign language. 'Who was it from?'

'A very old lady. She knew about Great-Uncle Tony's workshop being found, and she wants to buy all the tricks. She's says she's very rich. Dad?'

'Yes?'

'Have you ever wanted to be rich?'

'Such an ambition has never come within the compass of—' His father stopped and cleared his throat.

'I mean to convey that I have always engaged in wider considerations than—' He cleared his throat again.

'No,' he said simply. 'There are more important things than money.'

In the brief silence Stuart heard April shouting his name from the back garden.

'Can I go and see her?' he asked, and instead of saying something like, 'You have my unconditional assent,' his dad just smiled and replied, 'Yes,' and Stuart thought, with a burst of pleasure, how much simpler life would be if his father stuck to this new way of talking.

The fence between the gardens always made Stuart feel especially short; it was too high for him to see over, whereas April was tall enough to comfortably rest her chin on it.

She was standing on her side of the fence, sucking a bright blue ice-lolly. 'Hello,' she said. 'You look all weird and excited about something. What's going on?'

'Well, I had this mysterious phone call and—'

The entire top of April's lolly broke off in her mouth and she let out a piercing scream.

Stuart stared at her.

'It's *cold*,' she wailed madly, hopping from foot to foot. 'My teeth have gone all *tingly*. Ooooh! It's like pins and needles only in my teeeeeeeth!'

Stuart folded his arms. 'You're not April,' he said.

'What?'

'She wouldn't make a fuss about something like that. You must be May.'

Instantly April popped up from where she'd been hiding behind the fence, next to her sister.

'Very good,' she said. 'We were just testing you. I lent May my glasses and then I hid.'

May laughed. Stuart felt a bit irritated. 'What did you want anyway?' he asked.

'To tell you that I can't be at the museum tomorrow morning. We've got to go shopping for school shoes.'

'OK.'

'Bye, then.' She walked away, and May trailed after her, still complaining about her teeth.

Stuart watched them go, and then jumped violently as the third triplet suddenly bobbed up from behind the fence.

'Hi,' she said, grinning. 'I was hiding too. Did you like our test?'

'Not much. But at least I got it right.'

'Half right. The one with the lolly was May, but the other one was June. *I'm* April. You missed a vital clue.'

'What?' asked Stuart.

'June isn't as curious about things as I am. She didn't ask you all about the mysterious phone call, whereas I would have. It's about *what* we say, as well as *how* we say it.'

'Oh.'

'Maybe, if you really concentrate, you'll get all three of us next time.' She leaned her chin on top of the fence and smiled down at him. 'So what *was* the phone call about?'

'It was, um . . .' Suddenly he didn't feel much like telling her; he wanted a bit more time to think about Miss Edie's offer and what it might mean. *Rich with a great big golden capital R . . .* April wouldn't spring silly tests on him, and then lecture him on the result, if he had pots and pots of money – she'd be too busy wondering whether she was going to get a lift in his new car. He imagined the triplets trudging to school in torrential rain while he swished by in his chauffeur-driven Rolls-Royce. 'Sorry,' he said. 'There's no time to tell you now – it'll have to wait till tomorrow afternoon.'

'OK.' She looked disappointed. 'See you then.'

'See you.'

'Oh, hang on, Stuart. I had a brainwave about the Fan of Fantasticness. You know we'd decided that it must fold up somehow, but we haven't worked out how?'

'Yes.'

'Well, I remembered that May had this stupid plastic fan she won at a fair last year. When you opened it, it stayed open until you tried to stretch it out a bit *more*, and then it suddenly sprang shut. It broke after about two goes but I've done a drawing to show you what I mean.' She handed a piece of paper over the fence to him. 'I wondered if Great-Uncle Tony's fan might work in the same way. Only I think it would probably take two of us to try it – the mechanism might be quite stiff after all this time.'

'OK, I'll give it some thought.' Stuart pocketed the paper, gave her a grown-up sort of nod and went back into the house. An idea occurred to him.

'Dad, would you like to come to the museum with me tomorrow morning? I can show you how some of the tricks work and maybe you can help me with one we haven't solved yet.'

'A solution that needs lexicographic skill and cerebral— I mean, that needs word knowledge and brain power?'

Stuart looked up (and up) at the tall, spindly figure of his father, and shook his head.

'What we need for this one,' he said, grinning, 'is *muscle*.'

Chapter 17

The Fan of Fantasticness looked like a huge outspread peacock's tail, each of its 'feathers' made of silver metal enamelled with greens and blues. Stuart's father walked around it admiringly.

'Strictly speaking,' he said, peering over the top of it at Stuart, 'there is no such word as *fantasticness*. Although you'll find both *fantasticalness* and *fantasticality* in *The Oxford English Dictionary*.'

'I thought you were going to endeavour to use shorter words, Dad,' said Stuart. 'Both of those are even longer than the one I came up with.'

He unfolded the drawing that April had given him, showing how her sister's little plastic fan would ping shut if you tried to stretch it wider; and then he looked at the actual Fan of Fantasticness.

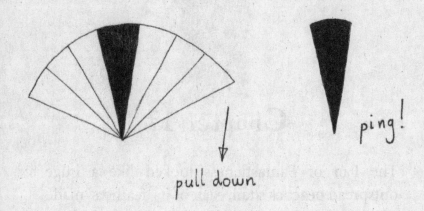

pull down

ping!

Each 'feather' was actually a very long thin triangle, joined to the others only at the bottom. It was obviously designed to fold up. And you could see that when it was folded, the triangles would all slide behind one other, with the one in the middle ending up at the front. And he also noticed that the one on the far right had a sort of ledge along the length of it. Perfect for putting a foot on, and pressing down . . .

Stuart gave it a go, and felt a slight springiness. 'Dad,' he said. 'Can you come round here? This is where I need a bit of muscle power.' His father wandered over.

'Put your foot on that ledge, next to mine, and when I count to three, really, really press down. As if you're trying to stretch the fan out even wider.'

'If you're confident that I won't contribute to its comminution.'

'You're using long words again, Dad.'

'Sorry. I won't damage it, will I?'

'I don't think so. Now – one, two, *three*!'

There was a rusty screech followed by the *boing!* of a giant spring, and Stuart found himself flying through the air. He had the weird impression that he passed straight *through* the fan before landing with a thud halfway across the room.

'Have you sustained any serious contusions?' his father called anxiously, loping across to where Stuart lay.

'No . . . I don't think so.' He sat up, feeling a bit bruised and dented. One of his shoes had fallen off during the flight.

'That's certainly an extraordinarily powerful mechanism,' said his father, helping him to his feet. 'One would have thought you'd been expelled from a cannon.' They both looked over at the Fan of Fantasticness. It had snapped shut like a Swiss Army knife. From where they were standing, only the central triangle was visible – all the other segments had folded in behind it.

'From several to single,' remarked his father. 'Rather akin to my continuing attempt to move from polysyllabic to monosyllabic speech.'

Stuart limped across the room to pick up his shoe. Odd bits of loose change from his pockets were scattered across the floor, as well as the remains of a packet of mints that he'd forgotten about, and he crawled around collecting them.

'My goodness,' said his father, peering into the mechanism of the fan. 'There's a considerable gap just behind this central segment. I think you may have passed through it during your flight. It's actually large enough for an individual to interpolate themselves into it – indeed, someone shorter than myself standing here would be totally invisible to the audience.'

Stuart looked up and laughed to see his father's head poking over the top of the triangle.

'That must be how they did it,' he said. 'Great-Uncle Tony's assistant would hop into the gap just as the whole thing snapped shut. Everyone would think she'd disappeared.'

'And there's an artefact here as well,' remarked his father, crouching down.

'A what?'

'A man-made object. One might call it a star – apart from the fact that it only has four extrusions.'

Stuart's hand flew to his pocket. The Magic Star had been in there; it must have fallen out when he shot through the air.

'And there's an odd quartet of sulci in the gap where I was standing,' continued his father. 'In fact, it looks as if this stellar object might be perfectly congruent with—'

A terrible realization shot through Stuart, and though he didn't know what the words *sulci* or *stellar* or *congruent* meant, he somehow *knew* that his father was just about to fit the four-pointed

Magic Star into a matching set of grooves that he'd just found in the Fan of Fantasticness, and he hurled himself across the room, arms outstretched, yelling, 'DON'T DO IT, DAD! DON'T FIT THE STAR IN THERE!' and had just managed to snag his father's sleeve with one hand when there was a soundless explosion, and he was no longer in the museum, but in a white, windowless room, standing on a blue and purple rug, looking at a painting of a volcano.

'*More magic*,' he said, his voice a whisper.

He looked around. His father was nowhere to be seen. The room was very large; it looked like something out of a stately home, with a massive fireplace, a grand piano in one corner, and three separate doors. It was full of sunlight, the white walls so bright that they hurt his eyes. *How can it be full of sunlight when there are no windows?* he wondered, and then he looked up, and heard himself shout in surprise.

There was no ceiling to the room. Above him stretched a clear blue sky. The only visible object was a tall square tower with a balcony running all round the top of it.

'Hello!' shouted Stuart. 'Anyone around? Dad? Are you here somewhere?'

There was no answer.

He walked over to the nearest door and opened it. It led to a concrete cell, bare except for a mattress on the floor and a bucket of dirty water. There was no ceiling on the cell, either. He closed the door again and opened the one next to it. Beyond lay a long sunlit corridor with yet more doors opening off both sides. He walked along the corridor and chose a door at random. It opened into a stable, in which an enormous horse was furiously stamping its hooves. It swung its head round and glared at Stuart with fierce reddish eyes, and he quickly closed the door and tried the one opposite. Inside was a room with a trickling stream instead of a floor, and a set of stepping stones which split into three paths, each leading to another door. The sun twinkled overhead, the tall tower casting the only shadow.

Stuart picked his way across the stepping stones, and chose the left-hand door. It opened straight onto a blank brick wall. He let the door swing shut again, and stood there, thinking hard.

'It's a *maze*,' he said slowly.

And then he heard someone high above him call his name.

Or rather, half his name.

'Stu!'

He looked up, startled.

Way above him, on the balcony at the top of the tower, stood his father.

Chapter 18

'Hi, Dad!' yelled Stuart, waving. 'Are you all right?'

Rather hesitantly, his father waved back. 'This is most odd,' he called down, his voice faint with distance. 'What is this place and how did I get here?'

Stuart tried to think of a simple way of explaining the vast and complicated truth, and then decided that he couldn't. 'You're in a dream,' he yelled. 'A very peculiar dream. Can you get down from there?'

'There's a steep set of stairs with a door at the base but the door has a bolt that is not on my side. I'm stuck here, I think.'

His father sounded disorientated and a bit wobbly, and Stuart realized that he would have to take charge himself; after all, it was his third magical adventure – he should know something about it by now. 'Dad, can you see I'm in a sort of weird maze?'

'Yes.'

'Can you work out which way I should go? You must have a really good view from up there.'

There was a pause while his father peered down, moving his head as if following a path. He walked right round the balcony at the top of the tower, disappearing from view for a few seconds, before reappearing and calling down to Stuart.

'Yes, I think I can see where you should go. You would end up at the foot of this thing.'

'What thing?'

'This thing that I'm on. This tall thing.'

'The tower, you mean?'

'Yes.'

Stuart stared up at him. He couldn't see his father's expression from this distance, but it was clear that something was very wrong.

'Why didn't you say *tower*?' he asked.

'I can't,' said his father.

'Why can't you?'

'I just can't. It seems that in this dream my mouth won't say words that have more than one . . . bit to them.'

'Bit?'

'Yes.'

'You mean syllable? You can only say one-syllable words?'

'Yes. *Yes*.'

His father's voice was full of frustration, and it occurred to Stuart that it was probably as hard for him to use only short words as it would be for Stuart to use only enormously long ones. 'Don't worry,' he yelled reassuringly, 'it's just part of the dream. It shouldn't be a problem – you just have to say left or right or whatever. Where do I go now?' He was still standing on the stepping stones in the room full of water, with three doors ahead of him.

His father peered over the balcony. 'Go through the door!' he shouted, and then paused to think. 'The door that is not on the left or the right.'

Stuart walked forward and opened the middle door.

A huge shiny green leaf barred his way. He pushed it aside and found himself in an enormous conservatory full of tropical plants, with creepers dangling from wires above him and vast, perfumed flowers blooming on every side. When he looked down, he could see a muddle of narrow brick paths snaking through the vegetation, crisscrossing each other in a complicated network.

'Which way do I go?' he shouted up to his father.

'To a door near a thing.'

'A thing? What sort of thing?'

'A thing from which clear stuff that you can drink comes out of.'

'Water, you mean? So I've got to find a tap? Or a hose?'

'No. You can find things like this in parks. A round shape. Splish, splash. Coins are thrown in.'

'A *fountain*?'

'Yes.'

Stuart moved cautiously through the vegetation. Butterflies flickered between the flowers; a lizard appeared, paused briefly on a bunch of nearly ripe bananas and then zipped away again Somewhere to his left he could hear the tinkle of water. He ducked under a hairy stem, parted a wall of leaves and found himself beside a stone fountain, with a jet of water shooting upwards out of the mouth of a stone dolphin.

On the wall nearby, almost covered with purple flowers, he could just see the outline of a door.

'Through here?'

'Yes. But take care.'

'Why?'

'In the next room there is a . . . a large beast.'

'Another horse?'

'No. It's huge and grey with a trunk.'

'You're not *serious*?'

Stuart opened the door just a crack and saw a square concrete room, the floor covered with straw. Lying across most of it was an elephant. It appeared to be asleep, though its stomach was rumbling gently, and occasionally it moved its trunk around, sending blasts of warm grassy breath across the room. Hardly daring to breathe, Stuart eased his way in and tiptoed forward, straw crackling underfoot. He felt even smaller than usual, and incredibly vulnerable. The elephant would only have to roll over, and he'd be flattened like a lump of pastry under a rolling pin.

Two metal doors lay ahead, one of them to the left and one to the right.

'You need to go through the right-hand door,' shouted his father.

'I can't,' called Stuart, as loudly as he dared. 'There's an elephant lying in front of it.'

Its vast bottom was actually wedged right up against the correct door.

'The door on the left is a dead end,' said his father. 'But if you go back to the plant room you could fetch some fruit which might tempt the beast to move.'

'Bananas!'

It didn't take Stuart long to locate the bunch where he'd seen the lizard, and he twisted off a handful and found his way back to the next room.

He held one of the bananas near the tip of the trunk, and the elephant groped forward sleepily, opening one eye.

'Bananas!' said Stuart, moving it further away. 'Come and get your lovely bananas!'

The elephant hauled itself slowly to its feet and Stuart threw the bananas into the far corner, then dodged round the side of the lumbering animal. The door was now clear and he made a lunge for it.

Chapter 19

He stepped into a long room with a cool, green marble floor, and walls hung with large paintings. It took him a moment or two to realize that the only door was the one he'd just walked through.

'This is a dead end,' he shouted up to his father.

'No it's not – there are . . . one more than ten ways out.'

'Eleven? Eleven doors? Where?'

'They're by the square things . . . I mean, not *by* . . . and not square . . . Oh dear, this is so hard to say.'

'You're doing fine,' shouted Stuart encouragingly. 'Have another try.'

'The things with *paint* on,' called his father.

'You mean the paintings?'

'Yes. The doors are not in *front* of them.'

'Behind, then? You mean the doors are behind the paintings? Or do you mean the doors *are* the paintings?' He walked up to the nearest one, a soppy portrait of a girl holding a box of chocolates, and yanked at the right-hand side of the frame. It swung straight open, just like a door, to reveal a hole in the wall, big enough to step through. And on the other side of it was a sweet shop, a really fantastic one, every shelf laden with jars, every counter stuffed with fudge and bubble gum and toffee and marshmallow and liquorice and chews and sherbet and fizz-bombs . . .

'Is this the way?' shouted Stuart hopefully.

'No.'

'Oh.' Disappointed, Stuart let the painting swing shut again. 'Which one should I go through, then?'

'The one that shows a . . . a . . .'

'I might as well try all of them,' said Stuart.

'No, don't do—'

'It'll be just as quick.'

He tugged at the frame of the next painting along, a seascape with a giant squid sticking its head above some improbably huge waves, and the picture smacked open as if on a spring. A torrent of freezing water gushed through the hole, and Stuart, soaked and gasping from the cold, struggled to close it again. A jellyfish flobbed through the gap, followed by a long, orange, sucker-covered tentacle.

'OUT!' shouted Stuart, using all his strength to slam the picture against the intruder. The tentacle withdrew, the door closed, and a sheet of water, green with seaweed, glided along the floor of the gallery, leaving a thin coating of sand behind it.

'OK,' said Stuart, teeth chattering with shock, 'maybe not such a great idea.'

'Are you all right?' called his father.

'Yes, just about.'

He had a sudden memory of assuring his mother that he and his dad would be absolutely *fine* while she was away, and then he looked at the next painting – an arctic landscape with a snarling polar bear – and decided to leave well alone.

'The one you want,' called his father, slowly and carefully, 'shows a room at the top of a house.

A room in the roof with things in it of all types, shapes and sorts.'

'An attic,' said Stuart.

He jogged around the gallery and soon spotted the painting he needed. It showed a dimly lit room piled high with bags and boxes; an old rocking horse stood in the corner. He pulled at the frame, and the painting swung open to reveal a similar room but one so stuffed with objects that it was actually difficult to see where he could climb in.

He eventually squeezed into a narrow space between a large trunk, a doll's house and a stack of hat-boxes, and began to edge around, coughing slightly at the dust he'd raised.

'I can't see a thing,' he shouted. 'There's too much junk in here. Where's the next door?'

'To your right,' called his father. 'To the back of the rolled-up red rug. Half way up the wall.'

When Stuart eventually spotted it, he saw that it was more of a hatch than a door – the sort of hatch that in a house would lead to a water tank – but it looked easily wide enough for him to get into. He pulled at the handle.

'It's locked!' he shouted up at his father.

'Oh.'

'There's writing on it,' called Stuart, pushing aside a cobweb obscuring the top of the door, and then groaning. 'It says, *The key is hidden in this room*.' He looked around despairingly.

There was a cardboard box right next to him, and he lifted the flaps at the top and glanced at the jumbled contents – some old light bulbs, odd tools, nails, tangled string, a loose pack of cards, a clock, a bag of curtain fittings: it would take him twenty minutes to go through this alone, and the room had forty or fifty other boxes, suitcases, bin-bags and bits of furniture. There were a million places to hide a key.

He turned back to pull at the door again, just in case he could wrench it open by force, and as he grabbed the handle, the rest of the cobweb fell down.

'There's more writing,' shouted Stuart, frowning at the peculiar collection of words in front of him, 'but I don't know what it means. And you can't say anything longer than a syllable so you won't be able to explain it to me.'

'I can try,' replied his father. 'Read it out.'

'OK. It says: *Cipher in mazarine coffret nigh pigmean demesne.* I wonder if it's a code?'

His father laughed.

'What?' asked Stuart.

'It's not a code. The words are rare and old, just the sort I like best. They mean: *The key is in a small blue box near the doll's house.*'

'Really?' Stuart scrambled to get it. The blue box rattled as soon as he picked it up, and he took out the key.

'And the next room is the last,' shouted his father triumphantly.

Stuart turned the key, opened the hatch and looked through. Everything was grey: a long, very narrow room, like a corridor, with grey walls, a smooth grey floor . . . and a grey ceiling made of a billowing fabric that bunched and shuddered in the breeze.

'A strange thing,' called his father; his voice was muffled by the cloth.

'I know,' said Stuart. 'It's got a *ceiling.*' At the very far end of the room was another door, and he could see a heavy bolt near the top of it. He wondered instantly if he'd actually be able to reach the bolt – though he could always come back to the attic room and fetch a box to stand on.

He wriggled through the hatch and dropped to the floor. It felt rubbery and slightly springy. He started to walk towards the far door, and he'd only gone a few steps when the whole floor began to move *backwards* – smoothly, like a conveyor belt. Stuart quickened his pace, but the floor speeded up as well. He broke into a run, and the floor whizzed along too, keeping him in exactly the same place, as if he were on a giant treadmill. Frustrated, he slowed to a halt again, and the floor stopped moving too. He was no nearer the far door than when he'd started.

'I can't get there!' he shouted. 'The floor won't let me.'

His dad said something in reply, but it was difficult to hear through the cloth ceiling.

'What?' called Stuart.

'Ape bars.'

'*What?*'

'Bars for apes. On top of the cloth.'

'I don't get what you mean. Shout louder.'

'PULL THE CLOTH DOWN.'

Stuart walked back, hoisted himself up into the hatch again, and reached upwards. He could just snag the cloth with his fingers.

'PULL IT DOWN?' he asked.

'YES!'

Stuart gave it a yank. The whole ceiling ripped softly away and fell in gentle folds onto the floor. And above it was a set of monkey bars, bridging the room from one end to the other. Stuart shouted in surprise, and then looked up at where his father stood, practically directly above him now.

'Did you say there are steps down the inside of the tower?' he called out.

'Yes.'

'See you at the bottom then, Dad.' Gripping the first rung, Stuart began to swing himself along – being good at the monkey bars was one of the few advantages of being small and light. It only took him half a minute to get to the door at the far end, and now he could see why the bolt was so high up – he could reach it from *above*, with one hand. He slid it loose, and at the centre of the grey door, a purple O suddenly appeared.

Stuart gave the door a kick. It opened inwards, but only a couple of centimetres. He gave it a second, much harder kick; it shot open, and hit something that sounded horribly like someone's head.

There was a groan and a nasty thud.

'Dad?' called Stuart, horrified. 'Are you all right?'

STRIGIL   HYPOCAUST

Chapter 20

'Mr Horten?' said another voice. 'Are you all right?'

Stuart looked round, and realized that in that fraction of a second he'd come back to the museum again, and April was peering concernedly over his shoulder.

He looked back and saw his father lying on the floor beside the Fan of Fantasticness, his eyes open and a red mark on his forehead.

'Are you OK?' asked Stuart, bobbing down beside him.

'That was so odd,' said his father. 'So odd . . .'

A cold hand seemed to grip Stuart's heart. Had his father's speech changed for ever? 'What was odd, Dad?' he asked hoarsely.

'I hallucinated that I was solely able to communicate in monosyllables, which led to considerable bafflement in my attempts to disseminate information to you. However, as I appear to have sustained a frontal cranial contusion, I was presumably experiencing a series of hypnagogic images which have now effectively dissipated.'

The cold hand let go of Stuart's heart again; his father was obviously going to be absolutely fine.

'You're right,' said Stuart. 'You got a bit of a knock when the fan folded up.'

'The Fan of Fantasticness?' asked his father, getting slowly to his feet.

'You told me that *fantasticness* isn't a real word. We should call it the Fan of Fantasticality.'

'But I thought you wished me to favour a more curtailed approach to vocabulary?'

'Shorter words, you mean?'

'Yes.'

'No,' said Stuart firmly. 'Definitely not. I want you to stick to the usual mad long stuff that I can't understand any of.'

April had been watching the conversation, her expression puzzled. 'What's been going on?' she asked.

Stuart grabbed the Magic Star from its socket and beckoned her over to a corner.

'Dad used the star,' he whispered, holding it up so she could see that there were only three spokes left.

'*What?*'

'Accidentally. And I caught hold of him and managed to go along too. Sorry, it was an accident – it happened when we were trying to fold the fan. And you were right about how it's done.'

He could see her struggling with disappointment. 'So what was the adventure like?' she asked, a bit glumly.

He thought for a moment; it was hard to describe it in the kind of words that he normally used. 'Peculiar, unpredictable, frustrating, extraordinary,' he said.

'You're sounding like your dad,' remarked April, managing a small smile.

The door opened with a bang, and Rod Felton strode in.

'Splendid news,' he said in his usual enthusiastic bellow. 'TV are interested. *Midlands at Midday* want to do a live feature on our special magical exhibition and they're sending a camera crew round in the morning. Can you be here at nine sharp?' he asked, glancing from Stuart to April.

They nodded, and then looked at each other. 'We're going to be famous!' whispered April, grinning with excitement. 'I must tell May and June,' she added. 'They can come along and report on it for the *Beech Road Guardian*.'

'And could you be here too?' the curator asked Stuart's father. 'Only I've had a rather brilliant idea about how to drum up advance interest in the Roman Beeton exhibition as well, and I need someone who can tell a strigil from a hypocaust.' He laughed as if he'd just told a joke, and Stuart's father laughed as if he'd just heard one.

'I should be honoured to assume such a role,' said Stuart's father, and Rod Felton bounced happily out of the room again.

'Actually,' said April, 'I've got another invitation. My mum says do you two want to come over for a barbecue this evening? Dad's cooking steaks.'

While April's dad filled the back garden with smoke, and May and June chopped up vegetables for coleslaw, April dragged Stuart into a corner by the shed and made him tell her every detail of the Amazing Maze.

'So the letters so far are S, W and O,' she said, and chewed her lip for a moment or two. 'And what about the mysterious phone call? You haven't told me about that yet, either.'

'Oh, right . . .' Stuart hesitated. The thought of that strange and tempting conversation made him feel uncomfortable. 'It was from a very old Canadian lady called Miss Edie who wants to buy all Great-Uncle Tony's tricks.'

'Why?'

'Well, that's the odd thing. She said she'd promised her grandmother, and that her grandmother had told her that Great-Uncle Tony hid a will in one of the tricks, leaving everything to the person who finds it, and—'

'Hang on,' interrupted April, flapping her hands. 'You said that this Miss Edie was really old.'

'Yes.'

'So when did her grandmother die?'

'Eighty-five years ago.'

'So before Great-Uncle Tony was even *born*?'

'Yes.'

There was a long pause.

'Did she seem a bit mad?' asked April tentatively.

'Not specially,' said Stuart.

'OK, well, let's ignore the grandma thing for the time being, it's just too strange. This hidden will, though – presumably it's the thing that all the letter clues are taking us towards. It said: *Lead you to my w—* didn't it, in the note? And I bet Miss Edie wants you to find it because then you'd be able to *prove* the tricks are yours, and you'd be free to sell them to her. But you wouldn't do that, would you?'

'Wouldn't do what?' asked Stuart, still flabbergasted (as ever) by how quick and clever April was.

She spoke again, her voice confident. 'You wouldn't sell your great-uncle's fantastic legacy – which you had to work so incredibly hard to find – to some woman you'd never met just because she offered you a bit of money?'

Stuart didn't answer. In his head he could still hear Miss Edie's crackly, insistent voice: *Being rich means you can get anything you want. What do you want, Stuart?*

Over by the barbecue, Mr Kingley was forking the steaks onto plates, and Stuart's father was setting up a table and chairs. May (or June) lugged a bowl of salad from the house, and June (or May) started pouring out drinks.

'Grub's up,' shouted Mr Kingley.

Stuart got to his feet, his stomach rumbling.

'I've just thought of something quite funny,' said April, following him up the garden. 'What if *I* found the will? Then the tricks would belong to *me*!'

Grinning, she went to sit down, but Stuart remained standing, and he wasn't grinning at all.

Though part of him knew that April was only joking, another part was seething with panic and jealousy.

They're mine, he thought, *not April's. They're mine to keep. And mine to sell.*

Chapter 21

When Rod Felton had said that a camera crew from *Midlands at Midday* would be turning up at the museum, Stuart had expected:

a)   a cameraman;

and, possibly,

b)   a soundman.

What he hadn't expected was:

c)   an assistant to the cameraman;
d)   an assistant to the soundman;
e)   a man with a bag of tools and three hundred metres of cable;

f)   an assistant to the man with the bag of tools and three hundred metres of cable;

g)   an assistant to the assistant to the man with the bag of tools and three hundred metres of cable;

h)   a woman with a clipboard and a stopwatch;

i)   a man with headphones and a beard;

j)   another man who introduced himself as the producer and then stood around doing nothing;

k)   a teenage boy who got everybody a coffee and then stood around doing nothing;

l)   a woman who introduced herself as the director and then wandered around anxiously doing nothing, but saying things like, 'I don't like the light in here,' and, 'How am I supposed to get my angles?' in a voice that sounded as if some terrible tragedy had just taken place;

and finally,

m)   a small dog.

For an hour Stuart and April stood in a corner and watched the producer and the director walk randomly around the room, pointing at things. They saw the assistant to the cameraman move a large lamp six times, before replacing it with a small lamp. They saw the dog investigate every single item in the room before lying down in a patch of sunlight and going to sleep.

'What's wrong with these people?' muttered April. 'They're so *slow*. Why can't they make any *decisions*?'

'Hi there,' said the producer, at last ambling over to see them. 'We're just waiting for our presenter to arrive. When she comes, we'll stick her in front of one of these trick thingies for the interview. Maybe she can sit on the big throne with all the flowers.'

'It's actually called the Reappearing Rose Bower,' said April.

'Is it?' he asked, not sounding terribly interested. 'Or we might go for that Wishing Well thingy. She could throw a coin in. Or maybe the red cupboard thingy with the swords.'

'You mean the Cabinet of Blood,' said April. 'They've all got names, you know. And seeing as you haven't decided yet, can I suggest you use the Fan of Fantasticality as a background? It's really beautiful when it's open, and we've worked out how to shut it as well. Do you want us to show you?'

'No, that's OK,' said the producer.

'It's no trouble. And it would definitely look really good. And the mirror arch is really impressive as well – maybe you could start with a shot of that, and then one of us could actually hide inside the Pharaoh's Pyramid and—'

The producer was beginning to look a bit irritated by April's stream of suggestions, and Stuart was just about to give her a nudge to shut her up when the door opened and yet another person came in.

This time it was a tall and glamorous-looking woman with glossy hair the colour of conkers, a cream suit, and shoes with heels so high that she was practically walking on tiptoe.

'*What* a drive I've had!' she exclaimed. 'I barely

knew that this town existed. Miles and miles and miles from anywhere!'

The producer hurried over to her, and so did the boy who got coffees, and there was some gesturing towards Stuart and April, and a fair amount of whispering. Then the woman came over to them, her heels clacking on the wooden floor.

'Hi!' she said, looking down at Stuart. 'I'm Rowena Allsopp.'

It was obvious from the way she said it that Stuart was supposed to know who she was. He glanced at April.

'Famous Midlands TV presenter,' muttered April out of the side of her mouth.

'Hello,' said Stuart. 'You're a famous Midlands TV presenter, aren't you?'

'That's right, and you're the one who found Tiddly Tom's magic tricks, are you?'

'We both did,' corrected April quickly. 'And he wasn't called Tiddly Tom, he was called Teeny-tiny Tony Horten.'

'And how old are you?' asked Rowena, not even glancing at April. 'Eight?'

'Ten.'

'Oh.' Rowena sounded a bit disappointed.

'I'm ten too,' said April.

'OK.' Rowena nodded, totally ignoring her. 'Let me go and have a word with my producer.' She click-clacked off again, and odd bits of the conversation floated back: '. . . see what you mean about the girl . . . more impact if the story's just about the small fellow – we needn't mention his age . . .' and then, rather faintly, 'I can't bear bossy kids . . .'

Stuart didn't dare look at April, but out of the corner of his eye he could see her turning pink. 'I was just trying to help,' she said, a bit huffily. 'I thought they should get their facts straight.'

Around them, things suddenly started getting busy. Rod Felton appeared, beaming at everyone. May and June Kingley sneaked in, May with her camera, June with a notebook. Plugs were plugged in, lights went on, the microphone was waved around, the dog was ushered away from the Fan of Fantasticality, where it had been sniffing interestedly, the producer shouted, 'Going live in three minutes,' and Stuart found himself shoved in front of the Well of Wishes, with Rowena beside him. Feeling half proud and half embarrassed, he grinned nervously at April, who was watching from the corner. She gave him a rather miserable thumbs-up in return.

'Counting down,' said the man with the beard. A red light blinked on the side of the camera. 'Going live in ten seconds. Nine, eight, seven, six, five, four . . .' He held up three fingers, then two, then one, then pointed dramatically at Rowena.

'Incredible as it may *seem*,' she said, gazing into the lens, 'the little town of *Beeton*, not previously known for *anything* of interest, has turned out to be the *hiding* place for a fantastic magician's *workshop*. The magician was called Teeny-tiddly Tommy *Norten*, and it was his very own *grandson* who made the dramatic *discovery* while watching a *talent* contest in Beeton *Park*. Here to tell us his incredible *story* is little Stuart *Norten*, who has gone from being a museum-hating *vandal* to being the *curator* of this exhibition.'

The camera tilted way down, as if it were filming

a beetle crawling on the ground, and Stuart looked up at it, no longer half embarrassed, but totally, completely and utterly embarrassed.

'I wasn't a museum-hating vandal,' he said. 'It was an accident.'

'So, Stuart, what *happened* when you found the workshop?' asked Rowena, talking to him as if he were a toddler.

'Well, me and my friend April saw that there was a notice board on the base of the bandstand, and we realized it was a bit loose, and when we looked behind it we realized there was a huge room underneath us . . .'

As Stuart told the non-magic version of the story, Rowena did a lot of nodding, but he got the feeling she wasn't really listening. Looking up at her was making his neck ache, so he dropped his gaze and saw the small dog sidling round the edge of the Fan of Fantasticality.

'And then,' he continued, 'I turned a wheel which I thought would open a door, and instead of that, the whole middle of the bandstand started to sink, and sudden—'

The man with the beard and the headphones started tapping his watch and signalling to Rowena.

'Wow!' said Rowena, interrupting Stuart in the middle of a word. 'That's *incredible*. Now let's talk to the chief *curator* of the museum, Rod *Felton*.' She walked past Stuart to where Rod Felton had been positioned in front of the opened Fan of Fantasticality.

'So, *Rod*, tell me the *impact* that having these fabulous items has had on your *museum*.'

'Well, Rowena,' said Rod, 'it's certainly an exciting find, one that's going to keep our summer programme ticking along nicely – but perhaps we should ask a visitor. Oh look!' he added, with obviously fake surprise. 'Here's one you could speak to!' He gestured rather woodenly to his left, just as Stuart's father walked round the side of the fan.

'Oh *no*,' muttered Stuart, wanting to crawl into a hole at the thought of his father on television.

Rowena shot a puzzled look at her producer,

and then managed a professional smile. 'Good morning, sir,' she said. 'Can you tell us what you think of this exhibition?'

'I would classify it as both serendipitous and recherché,' replied Stuart's father.

Rowena's smiled slipped a bit. 'I think what our viewers want to know is whether you enjoyed it or not.'

'An unequivocal affirmative to the former. But I am also ardently anticipating the forthcoming opportunity for examining our present conurbation in its pre-Saxon context.'

Rowena gawped at him. 'You *what*?' she asked.

'Aha!' said Rod Felton, stepping forward. 'You must mean the Roman Beeton exhibition, opening here at Beeton Museum in ten days' time – Tuesdays to Sundays ten a.m. to six p.m., except on Wednesdays when we close at three. Packed with interest for both the expert and the beginner! See you there!' He smiled and waved at the camera, resting one foot, in a relaxed sort of fashion, on the edge of the Fan of Fantasticality.

There was a loud *doinggg*, the fan snapped shut, and Rod Felton flew sideways through the air and knocked over Rowena Allsopp.

May Kingley's camera flashed.

'CUT!' shouted the producer. 'CUT! CUT! CUT! BACK TO THE STUDIO! Are you all right, Rowena?' he added, running forward.

'No I am *not*!' shrieked Rowena, struggling to her feet and dusting herself down. 'In my entire professional career I have *never* taken part in such a fiasco. Children who won't shut up, adults who talk total gibberish, amateurs who try to take over *my* interview, and now a vicious attack by a dangerous machine, all on live TV and watched by my *millions* of fans. *And* I've broken a nail and' – she frowned down at herself – 'and there's something on my jacket. Something wet. And there's a . . . a *puddle* on the floor just where I fell.'

Everyone looked down at the small puddle. Then everyone looked over at the small dog.

Rowena screamed.

'I am so, so sorry,' said Rod Felton.

'You *will* be,' said Rowena hysterically. 'The

whole of the Midlands has just seen me land, *live*, in a pool of dog urine. Apologies aren't good enough. I'm going to call my lawyer and get this entire museum shut *down*!'

Chapter 22

Stuart and the triplets stood in the corridor outside Rod Felton's office and listened to the row going on inside. Phrases like 'personal injury liability' and 'health and safety inspection' were being shouted really loudly. June was doing a lot of scribbling in her notebook. Stuart's dad had wandered off to the bookshop.

'They can't actually close the place down, can they?' whispered April.

One by one the camera crew trailed past them, lugging their equipment towards the entrance. The last one to leave was the teenage boy, balancing a column of coffee cups. A couple of metres behind him came the small dog. It was brown and white with a pointed muzzle and very short legs.

'*Shoo*,' said the teenage boy, turning. 'Go *home*.'

'Isn't it yours?' asked Stuart.

The boy shook his head. 'It followed us in. Must be a stray.'

The dog paused uncertainly, and Stuart watched as it turned and trotted back into the exhibition room. Something was tugging at his memory.

At the same moment the door to the office was wrenched open, and Rowena Allsopp stalked out, followed by Rod Felton, who had turned a bit pale.

He looked down at Stuart and April. 'Right,' he said, 'er . . . we've reached a useful compromise. Rowena won't sue us for criminal injuries and personal humiliation if we immediately close down the magic exhibition and replace it with a temporary display of her favourite outfits from *Midlands at Midday*. We've also agreed to stock copies of her brand-new biography, *Rowena's Way*, in the museum shop, as well as placing a full-size cardboard cut-out of her just by the till.'

Stuart and April turned to watch Rowena leave the building, the main door crashing shut behind her. 'On a brighter note,' added Rod Felton, 'she's agreed to come and open the Roman Beeton exhibition, which should get us quite a lot of publicity. She's going to combine it with a book-signing.'

'But what about Great-Uncle Tony's tricks?' asked Stuart indignantly. 'Where are they going to go?'

'Yes, you've put your finger on a *slight* problem,' admitted Rod. 'Our storeroom's pretty full at the moment. I wonder if one of the larger regional museums might take them until we've got some free space again. I'll start making some phone calls.' He went back into the office.

Stuart looked at April. 'What are we going to do?' he asked. 'If they end up in a warehouse in Birmingham or somewhere, we'll never get to see them.'

'Let me think for five seconds...' said April, screwing her eyes tight shut. 'Perhaps we could—'

'A petition!' announced one of her sisters.

'What?' asked April, opening her eyes again. 'What are you on about, June?'

'Save Beeton's Magical Heritage,' said June, making every word sound weighty and important. 'It's precisely the sort of thing the *Beech Road Guardian* should be doing. It's a matter of civic pride. We can print up a special edition – with photographs,' she added, looking at May, who nodded eagerly. '*And* I've got an idea for temporary storage of the magical tricks.'

'What is it?' asked Stuart, feeling left out.

June held up her hand like a traffic policewoman. 'No,' she said firmly. 'First I need to put down my thoughts while they're fresh in my mind.' She turned to a clean page in her notebook and started to write.

'And I've got some *brilliant* photographs of the whole dog-wee incident,' announced May, beaming.

April nudged Stuart. 'Shall we let them get on with it?' she whispered.

He nodded, but distractedly.

'What's up?' she asked.

'I've just remembered something,' he said, and walked quickly back to the exhibition room.

The dog was sitting on the bronze throne of the Reappearing Rose Bower, curled in a neat circle. It raised its ears as Stuart approached.

'What have you remembered?' asked April, catching up.

'I've seen this dog before. When I was in the desert, just as I'd managed to piece the pyramid back together, I caught a glimpse of it.'

'*This* dog? This *actual* dog?'

'I think so. And in Great-Uncle Tony's message it said that he'd 'lost an old pal', and *pal* means *friend*, doesn't it? So I'm wondering if this is who he meant. I mean, we haven't seen any *people*, have we?' The dog lifted its head and regarded them with anxious brown eyes.

'But in that case, how did it get out of the pyramid and into our world?' asked April, and then she clapped a hand to her mouth, her eyes wide.

'What?' asked Stuart.

'I've just remembered something too. When I was in the Arch of Mirrors, after I shouted all that useful advice to you about choosing the right reflection, the lights started to dim, and I could feel myself being sort of pulled back to the museum. And just as it got completely dark I heard something behind me. A clicking noise. Like little toenails on a hard floor, following me back to the real world . . .'

They both looked at the dog, and after a moment it twitched its tail in a half-greeting.

Stuart reached out and gave it a cautious pat, and it wagged its tail harder and craned round to sniff at his fingers. It occurred to Stuart that the last person to pat this dog had been Great-Uncle Tony. Its coat was warm and wiry.

'I've never had a dog,' he said. 'Only goldfish.'

'Stuart,' said April tentatively. 'Sorry to change the subject and all that, but since we've got a bit of time here, do you think we ought to make the most of it? After all, there's still three spokes of the star left. And that must mean three more clues – three more letters to find.'

Stuart felt in his pocket and took out the awkward little metal object. The next place it would fit was the throne of the Reappearing Rose Bower.

'You know we can't both go on this one . . .' he said.

April nodded. She clasped her hands in front of her, like someone being good in class, and Stuart could see that she was desperately hoping to be picked.

And he had an idea – a slightly mean idea, but a good one; an idea that would ensure he'd be the only one who found the final letter clue, and therefore the only one who'd be able to find the will.

'If you go on this adventure,' he said, 'when we get to the very last one, can I do it by myself?'

She gave a little hop of pleasure. 'Absolutely. Thanks, Stuart – and I'll be as quick as I can, because hanging upside down isn't very nice. Er . . . can I suggest something?'

'What?'

'Go to the loo before you strap yourself in there.'

Five minutes later, Stuart climbed onto the throne of the Reappearing Rose Bower and handed the Magic Star to April. 'Look after the dog, would you?' he asked. He could see it pottering around the room, its stump of a tail wagging briskly.

'Of course,' said April.

'And good luck.'

'Thanks. See you soon.'

She was grinning as he pulled the lever; the silver stems of the rose bower closed in a tangled thicket around him, and the metal strap snapped across his middle. He pulled the lever again, and managed not to yell as he spun upside down into utter darkness.

'You OK?' shouted April, sounding very far away.

'Mmmm,' was all Stuart could manage by way of an answer.

'I'll be off then.'

There was a little pause, an odd scuffling noise, and then a metallic clink directly above him. For a second the seat shook like the top of a washing machine on spin cycle, and then all was quiet again.

'April?' he called. There was no reply. She was in whatever world the Magic Star had flung her into. So now all he had to do was wait.

It was massively uncomfortable, the safety strap

digging into his stomach, the blood rushing to his head. He braced his arms and legs against the sides to take the weight off the strap, and wondered how long he'd have to stay there. He started counting, and got to 2,000 before losing track of the numbers.

Time passed. It was quite warm in the interior of the Reappearing Rose Bower, and despite his awkward position, he began to feel sleepy. He tapped out a couple of tunes on the metal walls, and then searched his pockets to see whether he had anything interesting in them. It took a bit of wriggling, but he discovered a fluffy boiled sweet, a paper clip and a peach stone. He dropped them, one by one, into the darkness. He wondered what the dog was doing. He wondered what his mum was doing. He tried to think of what the dog's name might be – Great-Uncle Tony's message had said it began with Ch: Chance. Chocco. Charlie. Charlie was a good name. Stuart yawned.

He was woken by his head banging against the side. The whole illusion was lurching, tipping, swaying, moving. It was being *carried*. He could hear muffled voices and the rattling of a metal roller door.

The Reappearing Rose Bower was set down with a crash, and Stuart banged his head again. The roller rattled down, a door slammed violently, an engine started with a deep growling note, and the rose bower jerked forward. Stuart banged his head for the third time, but he was panicking too much to think about the pain. He was panicking because it was clear that he was no longer in the museum but in the back of a lorry.

He was in the back of a lorry and he was being driven away.

Chapter 23

As April watched Stuart climb onto the throne of the Reappearing Rose Bower, pull the lever and disappear from sight, she clutched the Magic Star in her hand, and tried to keep her breathing steady.

One of the disadvantages of being a triplet was that she hardly ever did anything on her own – there was always at least one sister tagging along. Now she had the prospect of a whole magical world which she could explore without interference, and she felt almost dizzy with excitement. It took her a moment or two to realize that, mingled with the excitement, there was a good dollop of nervousness. It was always easier to be brave when you were with someone else.

She could hear Stuart pulling the lever again. The mechanism clicked and ratcheted, and the silver stems eased apart to reveal the empty throne. At its centre was the socket for the star.

'You OK?' she called to Stuart, and heard a vague noise by way of an answer.

She stepped forward, and at the same moment the dog skittered across from where it had been lurking and bounded onto the seat. It looked at her keenly.

'Do you want to come too?' asked April. The prospect of not being *quite* on her own was rather nice. 'I'll be off then,' she shouted, laying one hand on the dog's head and, with the other, placing the three-pointed star in its socket.

And, like a page turning, the view changed.

She was in the most splendid room she had ever seen. The bronze throne was still directly in front of her, but now it stood on a velvet dais, and red and purple silk banners swayed gently from the ceiling above.

The windows were high and narrow, and she

could see nothing out of them except treetops and wheeling swifts.

The walls were gold, and hung with tapestries, their colours brilliant and fresh: stags leaping through green woodlands, white castles standing in meadows jewelled with flowers.

The floor had a carpet so soft that her feet sank gently with every step; she reached down and stroked it, and it was like brushing the gossamer coat of a puppy.

Which reminded her of the little dog. She looked around and saw it had jumped off the throne and was sniffing around the edge of the room.

'What am I supposed to do?' she asked it. 'What's the puzzle?'

It was really odd not having anyone to talk to. She had the sudden wild thought that Stuart might have come with her to this magical palace, and she knocked on the throne and shouted, 'Stuart, are you there?' but there was no answer. He must still be in the museum, and she thought of him hanging upside down, getting cramp in his legs and nausea in his stomach, and she knew that she had to hurry up with her task.

As she turned away from the throne, she thought she saw a flash of movement out of the corner of her eye, but when she spun round there was no one there – or at least, no one *real*. There was a painting, though, that she hadn't taken note of before – a full-length portrait of a queen in royal robes, sitting on a throne.

She walked towards it, and again seemed to see someone moving, and her heart started thudding painfully. It wasn't until she was near enough to touch it that she identified the source of the movement. Instead of a painted face, the portrait had a small oval mirror set into the canvas.

Standing below it, April could only see a reflection of one of the windows, but a thought occurred to her, and she walked back to the platform on which the Reappearing Rose Bower stood. She climbed the steps, sat down on the bronze throne and looked straight ahead at the portrait.

And now it was herself – her own face, fitting perfectly into the oval mirror, above a painted body adorned with finery. A blue fur-trimmed cloak was draped over her shoulders, an enormous diamond ring glinted on one finger, a sceptre (like a golden rolling pin) was gripped in her right hand, an orb (like a cricket ball carved out of a giant ruby) in her left. On her head was a crown, the stones a brilliant green.

April grinned at herself, but the grin didn't really match the regal sternness of the pose. She tried a frown instead and it looked much better.

'Right,' she said, 'and *now* what?'

There were no obvious doors out of the room, but she remembered Stuart's description of the gallery he'd gone into, where every painting was a door, and she went back to the portrait and gave the right-hand side of the frame a sharp tug. It opened so quickly and smoothly that she almost fell over. She looked into the room beyond, and almost fell over again.

It was all flash and dazzle – a million facets catching the light, a blue blaze of sapphires, pearls like creamy gobstoppers, amethysts like blobs of blackcurrant jam, tigers' eyes, opals and rubies, emeralds the moist green of new leaves, diamonds like chips of shattered ice, and everywhere the warm gleam of gold, the cold glitter of silver.

A treasury.

A treasury that looked as if someone had turned the room upside down and given it a good shake, or else taken the roof off and stirred it with a giant stick.

'What a mess,' said April, out loud. 'What a complete and utter *mess.*'

She climbed over the parapet into the room. Priceless necklaces and rings with stones the size of grapes lay in tangled piles across the floor, rows of shelves around the walls bore stacks of random jewellery, and in the centre of the room, a tall gold candleholder in the shape of the sun was festooned with crowns and bracelets, as if it were a hat-stand. There were open chests crammed with treasure, chairs draped with it, a cabinet whose every drawer was stuffed with objects. There was even a small table off to one side where somebody had left a half-eaten slice of bread and cheese balanced on top of an absolute *pillar* of crowns, stacked up like a kid's building game. The cheese was the sort that her father adored – crumbly, streaked with blue mould and hideously smelly. And someone – probably the same person – had drunk some red wine as well, leaving the empty goblet on its side beneath the table.

The only object that wasn't completely covered with priceless items was a small footstool, standing on its own in one corner.

Something about it made April feel weirdly uncomfortable. She stared at it, fishing around in her memory, and realized after a moment or two that it reminded her of the Thoughtful Stool that April (or May, or June – but usually April) had had to sit on as a small child when she'd been naughty. *Stay there for five minutes and have a good think about what you need to change about your behaviour*, her mum had always said. Ever since, April had preferred to do her thinking at speed, and standing up.

She did it now, closing her eyes tightly, and – as usual – the solution popped almost instantly into her brain.

'The picture,' she said, with absolute certainty. 'I have to find the objects that are in the picture, and put them on. A crown with emeralds, a cloak with fur, a diamond ring, a gold sceptre, a ruby orb.'

Quickly she started to scan the room, and saw a diamond ring poking out of the coils of a pearl necklace on the floor nearby. She bent down to disentangle it, and then did a sort of screaming hop as a mouse shot out from underneath and zigzagged towards a corner of the room.

From the door in the wall came an answering yap, and the dog stuck its nose over the parapet.

'Thanks,' said April, scooping it up and setting it down in the treasury. 'Just keep the mouse away, would you? Not that I'm afraid of mice, of course – I just wasn't expecting it.'

Cautiously she had another go at untangling the ring, and realized that the pearl necklace was also wrapped around a crown – a crown with green stones.

'Two down,' she said, hooking the heavy crown over one arm and looking around for the next object, 'three to go. Easy peasy.'

It was at the exact moment she said the word *peasy* that she noticed another crown with green stones lying on the floor next to the candleholder. It looked exactly the same as the first.

'Right,' she said to herself, a bit less certainly. She moved her head fractionally and saw yet another one, right at the top of the tower of crowns on the cheese table. And a fourth on one of the shelves that ran around the wall. And she could see what looked like a fifth *and* a sixth hanging on a chair arm – and she couldn't help spotting at least six ruby orbs, several sceptres and umpteen diamond rings, twinkling amidst the golden chaos.

She took a deep breath. 'OK,' she announced to the room in a decisive voice. 'What this place needs is some organization. Fast.'

Chapter 24

She timed herself on her watch. Thirty-five minutes of non-stop action later, she had collected a total of fifteen emerald crowns and had stacked them in the throne room beside the Reappearing Rose Bower. Next to the crowns she'd assembled four other piles, consisting of nine diamond rings, ten orbs, thirteen sceptres and four fur-trimmed cloaks, all of which seemed to have moths. April stopped to catch her breath; it had never occurred to her that gold was so incredibly heavy.

'So now,' she said, 'I just have to find which ones are the right ones.'

She picked up the least mothy of the four cloaks and draped it round her shoulders; it was miles too long for her. Then she slipped on one of the rings, picked up an orb and sceptre, and finally grabbed the top crown on the stack and placed it on her head. Then, feeling as if she were a contestant in a fancy-dress competition, she shuffled across to the throne, cloak dragging behind her, and sat down.

Her own face, pink with exertion, looked back at her from the portrait.

Nothing happened.

'OK,' she said, 'let's try another lot.'

She took off the jewellery and the cloak and dumped it all to one side, went over to start dressing herself in a whole new set – and then suddenly had a thought. An awful, chilling thought.

What if she'd been wearing the right crown, but all the other items had been wrong? Or what if it had been the right cloak, but the wrong crown, ring, orb and sceptre? Or the right orb, the right crown, the right cloak and the right ring, but the wrong sceptre? It was no good, she realized, just randomly going through the piles – she would have to try on *every possible combination*.

'And there must be hundreds,' she said out loud. 'Maybe thousands! It'll take hours and hours and hours, and Stuart's going to be upside down in the museum the entire time.' She could feel herself beginning to panic; her insides felt cold and hollow.

'I must be doing it *wrong*,' she exclaimed, her voice a pathetic squeak. 'I've missed something – I *must* have.'

She ran back to the treasury, and looked around desperately. The dog was still nosing about; its stumpy tail wagged when it saw her, and April scooped it up and gave it a quick cuddle. And then, since she definitely needed to do some proper thinking (and not just closing her eyes and waiting for inspiration, the way she normally did), she picked her way between the piles of treasure, sat down on the little footstool right in the corner of the room and put her chin in her hand.

And saw something.

On the wall right next to her, directly underneath the lowest shelf, invisible to someone standing up, were five lines of writing.

CROWN CROWNING THE COLUMN
ORB ORBITING

RING AROUND THE RODENT ROUTE
SCEPTRE IN THE CENTRAL SLIDER
CLOAK CLOSE TO THE CLARET

Clues. Clues that she would have seen if only, at the start, she had sat down for just *one* minute. April's groan of despair sent the small dog leaping off her lap, and she buried her face in her hands. *Crown crowning the column* presumably meant that the correct one was the topmost of the huge pillar of crowns on the table. And *Cloak close to the claret* must have been the cloak she'd found on the floor near the tipped-over goblet, since 'claret' meant red wine.

But now it was too late – all the rings and crowns and cloaks and sceptres were completely mixed up and she had no idea which one was which. She would just have to work her way through every possible combination with as much speed as possible.

'Stuart, I am *so sorry*,' she muttered, standing up. She stepped over the dog, which was licking something on the floor beneath the table, and then she paused, and peered down.

The thing he was licking was a dried wine stain.

It only took her a few seconds to gallop back into the throne room and start examining the cloaks, and she jumped into the air in triumph when she found a small stain on the second cloak. She tossed it onto the throne, and sprinted back to the treasury, where she sat back down on the stool, focused on the clues, and thought deeply.

Orb orbiting.

Orbiting meant going round something. Like a satellite orbiting the earth. Or the earth orbiting the—

'Sun!' she shouted. There, in the centre of the treasury, was the golden candleholder shaped like the sun, and she'd found all sorts of treasure on it, including one of the orbs, balanced on a bracelet. She went over to the candleholder now, and noticed that odd drips of wax were scattered across the other objects on it, and then she made another dash to the throne room. It only took half a minute to find the orb whose ruby sides were similarly spotted with wax.

Ring around the rodent route.

Rodent = mouse, she thought.

So where had she seen the mouse go? She remembered that it had zipped across the room towards the tall gilded cabinet in one corner, and when she went over there and crouched down, she could see a tiny gap between the cabinet and the wall, and a trail of mouse poos indicating its usual route. But – and she felt almost certain about this – she hadn't found any of the nine diamond rings in this particular corner. She swept the patch of floor clean with one foot, then lay down full length and put her eye to the crack. And there, looking right back at her through what seemed to be a tiny circular picture frame, was a mouse, its eyes like drops of ink. It whisked away in a instant, and April was left looking at the miniature frame. And she realized what it was: a diamond ring, wedged sideways between wall and cabinet.

As she heaved the cabinet away from the wall, she was shaking; if she hadn't read the clues, she'd *never* have found the right ring. It tinkled to the floor, and she hooked it over one finger and carried on the search.

Sceptre in the central slider.

'What slides in this room?' she asked herself, and the answer was easy: a drawer. The cabinet that she'd just wrenched from the wall had five drawers – she'd searched it earlier and found at least two sceptres in there. She opened the middle drawer now and looked at the tumbled treasure inside. There was nothing to mark the contents – no wine stains, no wax – but as she stood looking, she saw a microscopic movement. A spider the size of a grape seed was dangling on a near-invisible thread between a ruby coronet and an opal bracelet, and April remembered something. When she'd taken one of the sceptres out of the cabinet, it had felt *sticky*, and she had brushed some grey thread off her fingers.

This time, as she careered from treasury to throne room, the little dog ran at her heels, as if joining in a game. It watched as she picked through the sceptres, and its tail appeared to wag when she found one with a swathe of cobweb still wrapped around one end.

'And now just the crown,' said April, an idea already forming. 'Do you like cheese?' she asked the dog. She went and found the slab of bread and cheese that had been resting on top of the stack of crowns, broke off a crumb or two and offered them to the dog. It hoovered them up. Then she arranged the crowns in a long line, picked up the dog, and carried it along the row, nose downwards, just a few centimetres from the crowns.

The dog sniffed violently at the fourth one, and when she repeated the exercise, going from the other end this time, the same thing happened again. Triumphantly she stuck the crown on her head, and hurriedly dressed herself in the enormous cloak. Then she put the dog under one arm, picked up the sceptre and the orb, and staggered over to the throne, feeling as if she were running a marathon. And she was just centimetres away from completing it when she tripped over the hem of the cloak, lurched sideways and dropped both dog and orb.

She flailed in the air, missed the dog, caught the orb, and landed on the throne on one hip, glimpsing her pink, horrified face in the oval mirror. Over it, a scarlet letter T suddenly appeared, and then the world gave a sudden shiver and she found herself back – *where?*

Chapter 25

In total darkness. In stifling heat.

She reached out a hand and felt a wall that was somehow soft and warm – a heavy cloth, she realized, draped right over the Reappearing Rose Bower, and she grabbed a fold of it and pulled. It slid away, letting in cooler air, and she saw that she was in a shed of some kind, with chinks of late-afternoon light shining through the plank walls, and odd shapes looming in the shadows nearby.

'*Oi!*' shouted a desperate, cracked voice from directly beneath her. 'Is that you, April? Are you back?'

'Stuart!'

She jumped off the seat, grabbed the Magic Star, and waited anxiously for Stuart to reappear. The lever clacked and ratcheted three times and the twining silver stems relaxed, revealing a small slumped figure on the throne.

'You were *ages*,' said Stuart huskily.

'I know. And I'm so, so sorry. But do you know where we are? Has the trick been stolen, or is this a museum store ... or what?' She was searching the shed as she spoke, and her fingers found and rattled at a locked door. 'And we can't even get out!' she added, trying not to panic.

'I don't know anything,' said Stuart. 'I've been under that throne the whole time, and I couldn't really hear what was going on. I know there was a lorry journey, and lots of moving around and crashing and banging, and then' – Stuart's mouth was so dry that his words turned into a series of coughs – 'and then it went totally quiet,' he continued, catching his breath, 'and it's been quiet for ages now.'

'But why didn't you use the lever to get out of there for a while?' asked April. 'Just for a quick explore, or some fresh air? I would have done.'

'Because I didn't know what would happen if you came back and I wasn't in the right place.' It had been so horrible and hot and claustrophobic, and his head had begun pounding so badly that a couple of times he'd nearly pulled the lever – his fingers had curled around it – but each time he'd had a dreadful vision of April completing her puzzle at exactly the same moment, and getting horribly squashed in the insides of the mechanism. 'I didn't dare, just in case something went wrong.'

'Oh,' said April. 'Thank you.' There was a pause. Stuart couldn't see her expression, but he could hear her taking odd, irregular breaths.

'What's the matter?' he asked.

When she spoke, it was in a very small, un-April-like voice. 'You're braver than I am,' she said. 'I couldn't have put up with that. I wasn't even brave enough to go on the adventure on my own. I took the dog with me.'

Stuart's stomach seemed to do a flip. 'You took Charlie? Where is he?'

'Still there,' said April. 'I tripped over and dropped him just as I was coming back. I'm so, so sorry.'

In the terrible silence that followed, there was the sudden sound of a key turning. Stuart jumped up and April stood tensely beside him.

The door opened.

Two identical heads were silhouetted in the low summer light.

'I told you so!' shrieked one of them. 'I *told* you they hadn't left that exhibition room.'

'May!' shouted April. 'And June! How did you find us?'

'How did you get in there?'

'How do we get out?'

'Where were you?'

'Where are we now?'

A million triplet questions seemed to fill the air, all of them unanswered, all of them incredibly loud. Stuart's head began to hurt rather a lot and he sat down again. The questions changed tack.

'What's wrong with Stuart?'

'Why's he so blotchy?'

'What's he been doing?'

'Are you all right, Stuart?'

'Do you need fresh air?'

'Are you thirsty?'

Stuart nodded to the last question, and one of the triplets ran outside again.

'Where *are* we?' asked April, for about the fortieth time.

'In the big shed in the corner of Dad's builder's yard,' said the other girl. 'It occurred to me that he might be able to store the tricks for a while, so I rang him up. And he happened to have a van coming back from a job, so they went straight to the museum and picked up everything. Rod Felton was very grateful.'

'So all the illusions are in here?' asked April. She pulled a tarpaulin away from some veiled lumps in the corner. 'They've dumped the Book of Peril on its *side*,' she said indignantly.

'What I want to know,' said her sister, 'is where you disappeared to. May waited outside the exhibition while I went to phone Dad, and she said that you never left the room. Obviously I didn't believe her because she's always such a nutcase, but when hours went by and you and Stuart didn't turn up, we came back to look for you, and now I realize that May was actually right. So where were you? And how did you get into a locked shed?'

April shook her head. 'I can't tell you,' she said. 'It's not just my secret, it's Stuart's.'

Running footsteps came from outside, and May reappeared with a mug and a large bottle of water.

'Here you are,' she said, pouring a mugful for Stuart. 'I filled it from the tap.' He drank the lot, and she poured him another.

'So, Stuart,' said June, looking stern and serious. 'I think it's high time May and I knew what was really going on. We've told your dad that you're working late at the museum, and we've told *our* parents that April's gone round to your house – not to mention borrowing Dad's keys without him knowing – and we're tired of covering for you both and we want to know the truth.'

Stuart glugged the second mugful of water and held it out for a refill.

'Because it's not fair, is it, if we keep helping you but you don't tell us anything?' said May screechily. 'It's not fair at all.'

He drank the third mugful, thought about a fourth, and then realized that he had begun to feel sick. Very, very sick.

'So come on, Stuart,' said June, folding her arms and using a phrase that she was ever afterwards going to regret. 'Spit it out.'

Stuart did.

SINGAPORE

Chapter 26

He didn't remember much about the journey home on the bus. He was feeling a bit like a strand of cooked spaghetti and lay limply across the double seat at the back, while the triplets looked at him anxiously.

His father, when he opened the front door to Stuart, looked even more anxious. 'I'm not sure whether or not to seek professional attention,' he kept saying as Stuart lay on the sofa with a cold cloth on his forehead, 'or whether this is a quotidian childhood ailment which boiled fluids, sufficient time and simple analgesia will alleviate.'

'What?' asked Stuart feebly.

'I am unable to judge whether it's serious or not.

I think maybe I should make a call to a medical authority.'

He disappeared for ten minutes, and then came back clutching the phone, which he held out to Stuart.

'Hello?' said Stuart.

'It's Mum. In Singapore. I've told your father not to panic.'

'Good.'

'Now, he said that you got very hot, had no fluids for the entire afternoon and then drank about a litre of water on an empty stomach. Is there anything else I should know, medically speaking?'

'I was upside down,' admitted Stuart reluctantly.

'When were you upside down?'

'Most of the afternoon.'

'Why?'

He hesitated. 'It was a sort of game.'

'Right. Well, I'm not surprised you're feeling ill. Stay cool, take lots of sips of water and have a good night's sleep. Get Dad to phone me in the morning if you're not completely better.'

'OK.' Stuart's mum was always very sensible and unpanicked about medical things. It was everything else that she worried about.

'Now, are you eating properly?' she asked.

'Yes. Dad's cooking lots of healthy things. Lots of them.'

'And are you having a lovely time with your new friends?'

He hesitated just a fraction before saying yes, and his mum noticed immediately.

'What's the matter?' she asked.

'I'm just missing someone,' he muttered, thinking about Charlie, wandering on short legs through a strange and magical world.

He kept thinking about the dog even after his mother had rung off – about how he'd first seen Charlie in the Pyramid, and then, later on, April had heard the click of his toenails in the Arch of Mirrors. Was it possible that all the magical worlds were linked? Could you go into one world and come out of another? And in that case, were there still two chances left to find Charlie?

That night, Stuart fell asleep early and slept heavily, and when he came downstairs – feeling slightly weak and extremely hungry – it was nearly midday. His father was in the living room, staring at a blank crossword puzzle while holding a spoon and fork in one hand.

'Hello, Dad,' said Stuart. 'I'm better.'

His father looked up in an unfocused sort of way. 'Excellent,' he said vaguely. 'I've just realized that *cutlery* is an anagram of *try clue*, so I'm planning an entire cipher based around kitchen utensils. Excitingly, the word *tine* has five different meanings beyond that of being the projecting prong of a fork.'

'Good,' replied Stuart. He went into the kitchen and poured some cereal into a bowl, and he'd just taken his first mouthful when he realized that there was a large brown envelope in the middle of the table, with his name written on the front of it.

Inside was a copy of the *Beech Road Guardian* and a letter in April's fantastically neat handwriting.

Dear Stuart,

I've got tons to talk about with you, but your dad says he's letting you sleep in so I thought I'd write you a letter instead. I hope you're fully recovered, by the way.

i) I'm really really sorry I took so long on the adventure yesterday. It was entirely my own fault for thinking of a solution too quickly - I have vowed to think more slowly and carefully in the future, and not to always assume that my first idea is the best one. Though it usually is.

ii) I've had an idea about the dog - you saw him in one place, and I saw him in another, so I wonder if he's able to wander around between the different adventures. In which case we might be able to get him back in the next one.

iii) The letter clue I got on the adventure was T, so that means we've got SWOT so far, which is a word for someone who works very hard in school. The only other thing the letters spell if you mix them up is TOWS, which doesn't seem to make much sense either.

iv) It wasn't till we got home last night that June reminded me I was supposed to be reviewing Clifford/Mysterioso the Magician's second magic show for the paper. We all went last night and the piece I wrote is in the paper (enclosed). It wasn't very good. (The show, I mean, not my review. Though I've tried to be kind.) The paper also contains a full account of the TV interview fiasco yesterday.

v) THIS IS THE MOST SERIOUS THING. Apart from the dog, obviously. And you being ill. Anyway, the most serious thing is WE ARE GOING TO HAVE TO TELL MY SISTERS because they won't give me the spare key to the shed in our dad's builder's yard until I tell them what's going on, so we don't have a lot of choice. But I promise I won't say anything until you say I can.

Yours sincerely – and sorry again. I'll call round
when you feel better.
April

Stuart unfolded the *Beech Road Guardian* and
looked at the huge headline that took up the whole
of the front page:

TV STAR THREATENS FUTURE OF BEETON
TREASURES AFTER UNLUCKY ACCIDENT

Midlands at Midday star Rowena Allsopp (says
she's 30, but looks older) had just finished
interviewing Beeton resident Stuart Horten
(10, but looks younger) about his recent
discovery of a spectacular workshop, when
museum curator Rod Felton (age unknown,
but looks about 40) accidentally triggered a
spring catch in one of the exhibits, leading to a
spectacular jacket-staining incident.

Turn to page 2 for full story by editor June
Kingley, with photographs by May Kingley. Turn

215

to page 3 for our PETITION to protect the BEETON TREASURES!

Turn to back page for other news and a review by our arts correspondent April Kingley.

Stuart turned to the back page. There was a small photo of Clifford, brilliantly spot-lit and holding the ace of spades in one hand and a confused-looking guinea pig in the other.

LIGHT FANTASTIC!

A small but expectant audience at St Cuthbert's church hall was rewarded yesterday with a bravura display of wonderful lighting, as well as some magic tricks.

ILLUMINATING!

The technical wizardry of electrician Elaine Coleridge (37) lit up a variety of illusions, including a partially disappearing guinea pig, a handkerchief that turned from green to red

216

and then from red to green again (twice), and a trick in which a member of the audience picked a card out of the pack, and Mysterioso the Magician (Clifford Capstone, 42) very nearly guessed which card it was.

BRILLIANT!

After the show Mysterioso the Magician described electrician Ms Coleridge as 'an inspirational genius'. 'I just wish,' he said, 'that my tricks were half as good as her lighting.'

Stuart suddenly had the feeling that someone was watching him, and he looked up to see April peering anxiously through the kitchen window. He got up and opened the back door.

'I didn't want to ring the bell and disturb you,' she said, 'so I climbed over the back fence. How are you feeling?'

'OK,' he said. 'I was just wondering how a guinea pig can partially disappear.'

'It was supposed to be hidden in one of Clifford's

sleeves, but it poked its head out through the cuff and started squeaking really loudly. Did you read my letter?'

Stuart nodded. 'I had exactly the same idea about the dog,' he said. 'We can go into the next illusion and get him back. As soon as we can.'

April grimaced. 'We won't be going anywhere unless we tell my sisters what's going on. They've got the key.'

Reluctantly, Stuart nodded. 'So when do you want to do it?' he asked.

There was a tiny tap on the window, and they both looked up. May and June were staring in at them, their expressions identically stony.

'How about right now?' asked April.

Chapter 27

Stuart went outside. 'OK,' he said to April's sisters. 'Get us into your dad's shed again, and we'll tell you everything.'

Both girls folded their arms. 'Truth first,' said one of them, 'then shed.'

Stuart folded his arms as well. 'Shed first,' he said, 'then truth.'

There was silence for a moment while they all glared at each other, and then there was an exasperated sigh from April.

'For goodness' sake,' she said, 'you all look *ridiculous*. Let's go to the café near the builder's yard and talk about it there. We can pool our pocket money.'

'But ...' Stuart glanced at May and June and

then turned and whispered in April's ear, '*But what if we tell them and then they still won't give us the keys?*'

April rolled her eyes. 'They're not a criminal gang,' she hissed, 'they're my sisters. They're just *nosy.*'

'We're *not* nosy,' screeched one of them. 'That's really, really insulting, isn't it, June? I feel really, really insulted by that description.'

'As editor of Beeton's leading local newspaper,' said June pompously, 'it would be surprising if I *wasn't* curious about unusual and interesting occurrences taking place in the area.'

April jerked her head at Stuart to indicate that she needed a word with him, and he followed her to the end of the garden.

'Look,' she said quietly, 'you don't have to *like* my sisters, you just have to *tolerate* them. That's what I do. So shall we go?'

Stuart hesitated, and then his stomach rumbled so loudly that even April heard it.

'What you need,' she said firmly, 'is a fry-up.'

*

At the café, Stuart had the sausage-bacon-double-egg-beans-fried-bread-all-day-breakfast special, which he ate with great concentration and in silence.

'OK,' he said to April, mopping his plate with the remains of the bread. 'I'm ready.'

'I have *never* seen anyone eat that fast,' remarked one of her sisters, looking revolted.

'Apart from one mouthful of cereal that's the first thing I've eaten since yesterday breakfast,' said Stuart indignantly.

'Well, don't blame me if you get indigestion.'

'I wasn't going to.'

'All right, all *right*,' said April, clapping her hands as if she were a teacher. 'Let's get started.'

She looked at Stuart expectantly, and he glanced over his shoulder to check that no one else in the café was listening.

'OK,' he said quietly. 'How it all started in the first place was that, right at the beginning of the summer holidays, I found eight coins and a note belonging to my great-uncle Tony saying that I should try and find his workshop. I started following clues, and then April helped me, but we discovered that they weren't just ordinary clues, they were magic clues – not guinea pigs out of hats, or handkerchiefs changing colour, but *real* magic, and—'

'There's no such thing as magic,' interrupted one of April's sisters firmly.

'There is, actually,' replied Stuart.

'No there isn't.'

'Shut *up*, June,' said April.

'Don't tell me to shut up!'

'You asked Stuart for an explanation and then you contradicted him after about five words.'

'Yes, but there's no need to be so rude. Don't forget that I'm the eldest.'

'Oh, don't start that again.'

'Yes, don't start that again!' wailed May, turning on June. 'I'm sick of being called the youngest just because I was born about ten minutes after April. And anyway, Mum says that actually means *I'm* the eldest, because I kicked you two out first and stayed till I was ready.'

'She only says that to make you feel better,' said April.

'Now you're *both* picking on me. It's not fair!'

Stuart rested his chin on his hands and watched them arguing. They were certainly easier to tell apart when they were cross: May got pink patches all over her face, and moved her head around twitchily, while June became very still and serious and upright, like a disapproving headmistress.

The bickering gradually ceased until they all sat looking at him again. 'Want me to carry on?' he asked. June nodded rather stiffly.

'OK, let's skip how it all started. Once we'd found the workshop, me and April discovered a sort of key inside one of the illusions. The key looks like a star, with six spokes. Every time it's used, it sort of unlocks a magical adventure with a puzzle to solve, and after each adventure, one of the spokes disappears.'

'What, you mean it goes *boof!* and vanishes in a puff of green smoke?' asked May, eyes wide.

'Don't be silly, May,' said June. 'Metal can't just disappear. It's a physical impossibility.'

'But Stuart just said it did.'

'Well, it can't.'

'Yes it can and yes it does,' said April, sounding exasperated and getting the Magic Star out of her pocket; it was now just a V-shaped piece of metal. She held it up and May stared at it, mouth open.

'But there are only two spokes left!' she exclaimed, outraged. 'That means you must have had *four* magical adventures already and not even told us!'

'There is no such thing as magic,' repeated June, not even looking at the star.

'Yes there is,' said April.

'No there isn't.'

'Is.'

'Isn't.'

With a loud chair-scrape, Stuart jumped to his feet and they all turned to look at him. 'Tell you what,' he said. 'The only way to explain this is to show you the illusions. Can we just go to the builder's yard? Please?'

There was a long pause and then June shrugged. 'We're certainly not going to get anywhere by talking,' she said.

As they were leaving the café, May took a copy of

the *Beech Road Guardian* out of her bag and placed it on the counter.

'What's this?' asked the owner, who was buttering slices of bread.

'Beeton's leading local newspaper,' said June. 'Would you like a copy for your customers?'

'No thanks, love.' He gave it a nudge with his elbow and it fluttered to the floor. Stuart picked it up and saw what he hadn't seen earlier – the article in the central pages about Rowena Allsopp and the TV interview. It was illustrated with three photographs.

Photo one showed Rowena standing next to Rod Felton, who was resting his foot on the Fan of Fantasticality. Stuart's dad was also in the picture, gazing into space with his unfocused 'inventing a crossword clue' expression.

In photo two, the Fan of Fantasticality had snapped shut, and Rod Felton was flying sideways through the air, just millimetres away from cannoning into a horrified Rowena Allsopp. Stuart's dad, meanwhile, remained in exactly the same position.

In photo three, both Rod Felton and Rowena Allsopp had disappeared out of the photograph altogether, apart from a blur that Stuart thought might be Rowena's elbow. Stuart's father was still gazing benignly into space, having completely failed to notice the colossal disaster occurring just to his right.

But there was something else in that third picture; something that caused Stuart to peer so closely that his nose almost touched the paper.

'What is it?' asked April.

He pointed.

When the fan snapped shut, a side view of the Cabinet of Blood had been revealed. The four elaborate swords hilts were silhouetted, sticking out of it. But in the middle of the dark cluster of sword hilts, May's camera flash had picked out a tiny, perfect, V-shaped gap.

'Brilliant!' exclaimed April. 'That's where the star fits next!'

Chapter 28

The builder's yard was open, and there was a lorry just inside the gates, into which two workmen were loading planks.

'You looking for your dad?' asked one of them as the triplets marched past.

'No,' said June, who had the keys in her hand. 'We're on a fact-finding mission.'

The shed was in the far corner of the yard. All the illusions (apart from the Reappearing Rose Bower) were still draped with heavy cloths, and as Stuart began to uncover them, it became obvious that they had been slung down rather carelessly.

Two of the mirrors in the arch were cracked, the fan was stuck halfway open, and there was a dent in the door of the Book of Peril. Worst of all, the Cabinet of Blood had been dropped on its front, and when Stuart and the triplets managed to haul it upright, he saw with a groan that all four of the sword handles were bent. He and April had never yet managed to remove the swords from the cabinet, and he imagined they'd have even less chance now.

'I'll go and borrow a wrench,' said April, dashing out of the shed again.

Stuart gave the cabinet a push to see whether it still spun, and it whipped round at a satisfactory speed, casting ruby reflections across the other illusions. Despite the array of scratches and dents, he felt a thrill of pride in his great-uncle's creations, and a sudden urge to show them off.

'We're waiting,' said June, tapping her foot impatiently.

'OK. Each of these tricks is a brilliantly engin-eered stage illusion,' he explained. 'For each one so far, we started by finding how the trick mech-anism works, and then that led us to the socket where the Magic Star fits. It all began with the Pharaoh's Pyramid.'

He pulled open the snake handle on one of the pyramid's sides and crawled in. 'This is really clever, this is. You'll see that, when I close it, I'll be able to escape out of the back by pressing a button in the floor.' He looked up at the pair of identical faces. One of them was looking stern, in a calm sort of way, and the other looked more excited, like a kid waiting for a pantomime curtain to go up – and he realized that, for the first time since he'd met them, he actually knew which one was which. 'You're June,' he said, pointing to the first, 'and you're May.'

'Yes, we *know*,' said May. 'You don't have to tell *us*.'

'And, actually,' added June, 'it's rude to point.'

Grinning, Stuart closed the pyramid door, waited for the luminous stars to become visible, and then pressed the button in the centre of the floor.

There was a nasty clanking, grinding sound – the sort of noise you get when a chain comes off a bicycle – and one of the pyramid sides juddered. A minute crack of light, the width of a hair, became visible. Stuart gave the side a light push, and then a harder one, but it didn't move.

'I thought you were supposed to be reappearing,' shouted one of the triplets.

'I've got the wrench,' he heard April say breathlessly. 'Where's Stuart?'

He leaned his full weight against the side, and the hair's-breadth crack doubled in width. 'In here,' he shouted through it. 'The side's stuck. I think it might have been damaged when it was moved. Can you try all the handles?'

He heard a series of effortful grunts from April, followed by a dejected, 'No.'

'I'll get a crowbar,' she added, disappearing again.

Stuart sat in humiliated silence until she returned a couple of minutes later and, with much heaving and levering, managed to prise open a gap wide enough for him to wriggle out.

June and May were standing with their arms folded.

'Well, that was really impressive,' said May. '*Not*.'

'Wait till you see how the Arch of Mirrors works,' said April indignantly. 'It's brilliant!'

She knelt beside the arch and flipped the fake mirror at the bottom. There was a loud snap, and she looked up at Stuart, white-faced, the broken mirror in her hand.

'It strikes me that there's evidence here of poor workmanship,' said June, getting out her notebook.

'It strikes me,' said Stuart, his temper rising, 'that there's evidence of the person who arranged for these tricks to be moved not telling the people who were moving them that they were fragile and should be handled with *care*.'

April got to her feet. 'Stuart, I'm really, really sorry.'

'It's not your fault,' he muttered. 'Let's see what we can do with the Cabinet of Blood. We've never even managed to open this one,' he added, for the benefit of April's sisters.

They went over to inspect it.

The four sword hilts were no longer all clustered together, as they'd been in the photograph, but splayed outwards. The neat little V-shaped gap that Stuart had spotted in the newspaper was now a space big enough to put a whole hand into.

Visible between the sword hilts was a tiny ring-pull, coloured the same ruby red as the rest of the door. Stuart reached up to tug at it, but at full stretch could only just hook the first joint of his finger through the ring.

April looked away tactfully while he struggled.

'You better do it,' he said, stepping back, and watched as she gave the ring a tug. Nothing happened.

'I can feel something when I pull it, though,' she said. 'It's as if I'm releasing a catch or a spring.'

'I've got an idea,' said Stuart. 'Do it again.' This time, when she pulled, he reached up and grasped the hilt of the lowest sword. And smoothly, easily (despite its bent handle), he drew it out of the door.

He reached up for the next, and April (with her other hand) took out the top two, and the door of the cabinet swung open. The interior was painted a dull gold, dimly reflecting their faces.

'So I suppose Teeny-tiny Tony's assistant would step into the cabinet,' said April, 'and then the door would close, and then Teeny-tiny would shove the swords back in.'

'Well, I wouldn't call that much of a trick,' said June. 'I mean, all the assistant would have to do is crouch down when the door's shut, and the swords wouldn't go anywhere near her.'

'Easy peasy lemon squeezy,' added May.

'So what's that then?' asked Stuart, pointing. Inside the cabinet, protruding from the back wall, were two gold loops like big bracelets, one at neck height for an adult, one at waist height.

'They're to make sure the assistant doesn't move,' said April. She hopped into the cabinet, stood against the back wall and clicked the lowest of the loops shut around her chest. Then she reached up and snapped the other one round her forehead.

'Go for it, Stuart,' she said, grinning.

'Are you sure?' he asked.

'Your great-uncle hasn't let us down yet, has he?'

'OK.'

Stuart shut the door of the cabinet, and there was a sort of squeak and then a giggle from April.

He picked up one of the swords.

'What on *earth* do you think you're doing, Stuart?' asked June, sounding more like a headmistress than ever.

'You still OK, April?' called Stuart.

'I'm fine.' April sounded surprisingly *near*, almost as if she weren't inside the cabinet at all.

'So shall I put the first sword in?' he asked.

'Yes.'

'Noooooooooooooooooooooooooooo!' screamed May, lunging forward. 'You're going to kill my sister! I *know* you're going to kill her!'

Chapter 29

'Stop immediately,' commanded June, grabbing Stuart's sword arm. 'I order you to stop.'

'Help!' screamed May. '*Help!* He's murdering April!'

The door to the shed suddenly opened, and everyone stopped yelling. The triplets' father was standing there, looking irritated.

'What's going on?' demanded Mr Kingley.

'Nothing,' said everybody. Stuart hid the sword behind his back.

'Then it's a very *noisy* nothing. Where's April?'

'Here, Dad,' she said. 'At the back of the red cabinet. Spin it round.'

Doubtfully, Mr Kingley reached out a hand and rotated the cabinet, and Stuart and the other triplets gasped as April came into view, standing on the *outside* of the cabinet, the gold loops still fixed around her forehead and chest, her heels resting on a tiny platform. She grinned at their startled faces.

'As the door closed, the whole back wall swivelled round,' she said. 'So it doesn't matter how many swords are bunged in, I'm actually completely safe.'

'*Swords?*' repeated Mr Kingley. 'Who's mucking around with *swords?*'

'As you know, Dad,' said June loftily, 'I'm not a mucking-around sort of person. I proceed carefully and methodically in everything I do.'

'And what about your sisters?'

'As the eldest, I'll make sure they do the same.'

'You are *not* the eldest!' screamed May.

'I promise we'll be careful,' said April solemnly and not very believably.

Her father sighed. 'Someone told me when you were born that girls would be less trouble than boys. To which I say, *Ha ha ha.*'

There was a pause.

'Please, Dad,' said the triplets, and then all three smiled hopefully at their father with smiles that were absolutely identical.

He rolled his eyes. 'Any more yelling and I take the key back. Stuart . . .'

'Yes.'

'I leave you in charge.'

Mr Kingley left the shed.

The girls looked at Stuart.

'I'm in charge,' he said. It was a brilliant feeling.

He helped April release herself from the cabinet, and they both pushed the swords back into the door.

'I am prepared to admit,' said June grudgingly, 'that the cabinet trick is quite clever.'

'But it's not actually *magic*,' squeaked May. 'Not *real* magic.'

April rolled her eyes. 'We've already explained about eight hundred times that you need to use the Magic Star to unlock the *real* magic bit.'

'Go on then.'

'Well, I don't know if we can,' said April worriedly.

Stuart was trying to push the bent sword hilts back together, to re-create the tiny V-shaped gap that he'd seen in the photo, but they were too far apart.

April tried to help, but the springy, twisted metal resisted their efforts. Minutes went by; Stuart could feel himself getting red in the face. 'It's no good,' he said flatly, abandoning the task. 'We can't do it,' and for once it wasn't April who contradicted him. It was June.

'We can,' she said.

'How?'

'Four swords, four of us. If we each push on one from a different angle, we've got a good chance of closing the gap.'

Stuart looked at April. 'June's right, you know,' she muttered.

Slowly he nodded. 'But think what that would mean . . .' he replied.

'What?' demanded May. 'What would it mean?'

'It would mean you'd both come along with us.'

'Along where?'

'Along to wherever we're going. Wherever the Magic Star sends us. The desert, or a hall of mirrors, or a weird maze.'

'Or a palace full of treasure,' added April. 'And once we're there, we have to solve a puzzle before we can get back. It's really amazing.'

'What if you don't solve it?' asked May.

There was a pause, and then May let out a squeak of horror.

'You mean we might all get *stuck* there?'

'Stop screeching, May,' said June, stepping forward. 'This is all made up anyway. There's no such thing as magic, and as a campaigning journalist, I'm prepared to prove it. And as a press photographer, you should be prepared to document it.' She placed a hand on one of the sword hilts. 'Shall we try?'

Stuart hesitated for a tiny moment, weighing the options. On one side of the scales stood the triplets, shouting, arguing, issuing orders, taking absolutely no notice of what he was saying (even though their father had put him in charge); but on

the other side was the next letter clue – and Charlie.
And small as Charlie was, the scales were tipping in
his favour.

'OK,' said Stuart. 'Let's do it.'

Chapter 30

All four of them grasped a sword hilt.

'On the count of three,' said Stuart, 'push them together as hard as you can, and then April can slip in the Magic Star. One . . . two—'

'Shouldn't April hold the star in place *before* we push?'

'What, and get my fingers totally crushed? Thanks very much, June.'

'It was just a suggestion.'

'A really stupid one.'

'I'm in charge,' said Stuart.

'Please don't call me stupid, April.'

'I wasn't.'

'That's what you were implying.'

'June was only making a suggestion, you know.'

'That's just typical – you always weigh in on June's side.'

'I do not.'

'May, I don't need you to defend me – I'm perfectly capable of defending myself. What I was saying to April was—'

'I'M IN CHARGE SO WILL YOU ALL PLEASE JUST SHUT UP!' bellowed Stuart.

There was an astonished silence. May and June's eyes were round with shock.

'Got the star ready?' he asked April. She nodded, and he could see that she was biting her cheeks in an effort not to laugh. 'On a count of three, then,' he continued. 'One—'

May raised her hand, as if she were in class.

'Yes?' asked Stuart wearily.

'I know you all think I fuss all the time, but I just wanted to point out that since this trick got damaged on the outside, how do you know it isn't damaged on the inside as well? The magic adventure might go all wrong and be horrible and scary instead of puzzling and exciting.'

'You can't accidentally *bend* magic,' said April.

'It's not like a *spoon* or something.'

'How do you know?'

'Because there's no such thing as magic,' said June, for about the fortieth time.

May looked a bit sulky. 'No one ever listens to me,' she muttered.

'Can we get on now?' asked Stuart. 'One ... two ... *three*.'

He was standing facing a brick wall, his nose almost touching the rough surface. Startled, he took a step back, and realized that there was a brick wall on either side of him as well, close enough for him to be able to touch both at the same time. He looked up, and saw that the walls were enormously high, and at the top of them was a white ceiling, brilliantly lit.

And then he turned round.

His first thought was that he was standing at the end of a bowling alley lane. Between the parallel brick walls stretched a narrow patterned pathway, curving gently up towards what looked like a set of battlements.

None of the triplets were in sight. 'Anyone around?' shouted Stuart. 'April? May? June?' He thought he could hear a distant reply somewhere to his left, but he couldn't make out the words. 'Charlie!' he called, and then remembered that 'Charlie' probably wasn't even the dog's real name. 'Champ!' he tried. 'Chester! Cheddar! Chumley!' There was no answering bark.

Stuart looked at the path beneath his feet. The paving stone he was standing on was plain white, but the next one was decorated with a large red circle, the third had a painting of a duck on a pond, and the fourth showed a blue and white teapot. The images were like the ones on picture dominoes: simple and clear. Stuart looked all around to see if there was any sort of clue for him to find, or read, or listen to, but there was nothing obvious. He stepped forward onto the red circle.

Instantly the entire paving stone shattered like a cream cracker and he dropped into water. Dark, freezing water – water so cold that, for a few seconds of frantic thrashing, he couldn't even catch his breath, and then he surfaced again, gasping and coughing, got his elbows onto the edge of the plain white slab, and hauled himself out.

He stood panting and shivering, his heart a drum-roll.

That was dangerous, he thought, staring down at the rectangle of dark water. *Really, properly dangerous.*

And then he thought: *What if May was right? What if the trick was damaged on the inside as well as the outside?*

The surface of the water was smooth now, and slate-grey. He could easily step right over it, onto the paving stone decorated with the duck, but now he was terribly afraid of what might be beneath it. And yet what choice did he have? He sat down, stretched out his legs, and gave the duck a couple of whacks with his heels. It seemed solid enough, so he stood up and quickly (before he could lose his nerve) jumped onto it. For a couple of seconds nothing happened, and then he realized that he was sinking – sinking very gradually into the stone, as though he were standing on treacle. The surface lapped up the sides of his shoes and began to close over his toes. Frantically he pulled up one foot, but the other sank deeper, and it was a truly horrible feeling, as if his leg were being swallowed by a giant throat. Stuart could feel it beginning to tighten around his ankle and he lunged forward, falling on his knees onto the next paving stone. His swallowed foot jerked free, minus its shoe, and he knelt, soaked and trembling, and waited for something even worse to happen. A minute went by, and then another. Water dripped off his clothes and pooled around him. The paving stone that he was kneeling on, with its picture of a jolly blue teapot, remained an ordinary paving stone, and at last he got to his feet. His squeezed foot felt all wobbly and feeble, and so did his brain.

From somewhere to his right he heard a shriek, and he called out, 'May, is that you?' but there was no reply.

He tried to gather his thoughts. The circle and the duck had been disasters, but the teapot was OK. Could it be a code? Or a visual crossword? 'Teapot,' he said out loud. Was there another word for a teapot? He didn't think so.

He looked at the paving stones ahead of him, each printed with a clear, simple picture, and he estimated that he could jump as far as the third, but no further than that. Which meant that he had to choose between a parachute, a cow and a leg.

'Chute. Jump. Fall. Milk. Moo. Udder. Limb.' The leg in the picture was bent as if about to kick a ball. 'Kick. Bend. Knee.'

Nothing seemed to make any sense, or to fit with anything else. 'Great-Uncle Tony,' he said. 'What were you thinking?' And then he knew.

The clue was in his great-uncle's name.

Chapter 31

Stuart looked down at his feet, and then at the third paving stone from where he stood.

'Tea,' he said, looking at the teapot. 'Knee,' he added, looking at the leg. 'Tea Knee. As in *teeny*. As in Teeny-tiny Tony Horten.' And then he took half a step back, clenched his fists, breathed deeply and launched himself into the biggest standing jump he'd ever done, landing with a thud on the rock-solid picture of the leg.

Eagerly he scanned the path ahead, looking for a picture of a tie. There wasn't one. Puzzled, he looked again at the next three images: a pie, a pig and a fork. The pig was standing behind a fence. 'Tea Knee Sty-ny Tony Horten?' he muttered. 'Tea Knee Pie-ny?' And then he gazed at the fork and remembered his father's lecture on cutlery. What were the prongs of a fork called?

Tines.

'Tea Knee Tine,' he said, and gave a confident leap across to the third paving stone. The next two were plain white, and he shuffled across them cautiously, feeling relieved to be on a little island of safety. He was feeling warmer now, and a bit more confident. He wondered how the triplets were getting on. He hadn't heard any shrieks for a while; he wasn't sure whether that was a good or a bad thing.

'April?' he shouted. 'Can you hear me?

There was no reply.

'Right,' he said to himself. 'I'm looking for the letter E.'

And it was there, on the very next paving stone. Except that it was a rather curly-looking E that could equally well (he decided, looking at it sideways) be a 3. Or even an M. Or a W.

He gave the stone with the curly E a jab with his foot, and a hole instantly opened up. A vile-smelling black goo began to slide out of the gap, and Stuart jumped back hastily. Holding his nose, he craned to see the next two paving stones. He could make out a compass and a flamingo. Neither seemed to have any connection with the letter E. The black slime was still pouring steadily out of the hole, forming large bubbles which popped with the noise (and smell) of a particularly horrible fart. Stuart took another step back, and tried to think.

Compass.

Flamingo.

The goo spluttered and oozed towards him. Stuart took yet another step back, thinking that it was lucky he had the mini-island of three paving stones to retreat to – and then it occurred to him that with such a long run-up, he could jump much further than before – he could reach the fourth, or even the fifth stone ahead. The trouble was that from this distance it wasn't so easy to see the images.

The fourth flagstone was printed with an orange elephant but the fifth was covered in rows and rows of little pictures like hieroglyphs, of which he could only make out one or two of the nearest – a windmill, and what looked like a yo-yo, and a zebra. The black goo was beginning to flow over his feet as he dithered over the clues. Elephant began with an E but it couldn't be that easy, could it? Flamingos laid Eggs. One of the points of the compass was East. And what were all the little pictures about? What did a windmill and a yo-yo have in common with a zebra?

Suddenly he smacked his forehead in realization. The *alphabet*, of course. And now he could see there was a gap in the top row of the little pictures. One letter was missing, and he just *knew* which one it would be.

Hastily he backed off as far as he could, and then sprinted forward, fists clenched, legs pumping. His intention was to launch himself like an Olympic long-jumper, but the last couple of steps of his run-up were taken through the overflowing slime. One foot slid, then the other, and instead of pedalling majestically into the air, he found himself lurching forward like a flung pancake. He belly-flopped to the ground.

Cautiously he opened his eyes a crack, and saw the little alphabet pictures just a couple of centimetres from his face. *Apple*, *ball*, *chair*, *dog*, *fish*, *grapes* . . . Which meant that the top half of his body was on the right paving stone. He moved one of his legs, and then the other; the surface they were resting on seemed to be tipping, and with a burst of panicky speed, he scrabbled to safety.

He sat up and looked back.

The elephant paving stone had swung open like a revolving door, one side of it sticking straight up in the air, the other pointing downwards into a deep, dark hole. Stuart peered into it, and saw a set of narrow steps spiralling into the depths. If he'd missed his footing he could have broken his leg, or worse. A smell of ancient damp wafted out of the hole, and he stood up hastily, eager to get away. The path was climbing quite steeply now, and he noticed that the walls on either side of him were lower too, so that there was a gap between the top of them and the ceiling.

'OK,' he said, scanning the paving stones ahead, 'so I've done Tea Knee Tine E. And now what I need to find is a picture of a—'

'TONE!' shouted someone on the other side of the wall to his right.

'April?' called Stuart. He'd never been so pleased to hear someone's voice in his life. 'It is April, isn't it?'

'Yes! Hooray, I'm sick of being on my own and I'm really, really worried about my sisters. I've been keeping track of May's shrieks, but I haven't heard June at all. This place is frightening.'

'Did you fall in the water?'

'Yes. And one of my shoes got swallowed up and my feet are covered in that vile, disgusting black slop, and I nearly fell down that staircase under the elephant stone.'

'Me too. I did exactly the same thing!'

'Great minds think alike.'

'You haven't seen the dog, have you?'

'No,' she said dolefully. 'Not yet.'

'So where do we go now?' he asked, looking at the next three pictures. They showed a loaf of bread (*Teeny-tiny Dough-ny Horten?*), a needle and thread (*Teeny-tiny Sew-ny Horten?*) and a series of stripes, shading from white, through pink, to red (*no idea*).

'I've already worked it out,' called April. 'It's the third one.'

'How does a set of stripes represent *Toe*?'

'It doesn't. It represents *Tone*. As in *tones of the same colour*.'

'Are you sure?'

'Absolutely certain. I'm already standing on it.'

Despite everything, Stuart actually laughed. 'I thought you said you were going to stop making snap decisions.'

'I'm in a hurry. Come on!'

'OK.' He made the jump.

Tea Knee Tine E Tone.

There wasn't far to go now: the path was curling up towards a terrace, and the walls were shrinking with every step.

'Right,' shouted April. 'A mountain, a donkey and a light bulb.'

'E for Everest?' suggested Stuart.

'Or the formula for the speed of light?'

'Huh?'

'E equals mc squared?'

'Might be, I suppose.'

'Shall I try?'

'Hang on,' said Stuart, before April could go leaping off again. 'Why's the donkey got its mouth open?' It was a fat, jolly-looking donkey, its mouth wide open and its head tipped back.

'It's braying, I suppose,' said April doubtfully.

Stuart nodded slowly. 'You're right,' he said. 'It is braying. It's going, *Hee-haw.*'

There was a pause, and then they both spoke in unison.

'*Tea Knee Tine E Tone Hee Haw.*'

'Brilliant!' shouted April. 'Nearly there.'

They both leaped onto the donkey stone at the same time, and Stuart's saw April's head bob briefly above the wall.

'There's a white one after the light bulb,' said Stuart, jumping again.

And now there were only three more patterned paving stones, and after that, a set of steps leading up to the parapet.

'So what do you think?' he asked, looking at the last three pictures. The first was marked with a large green X, the second showed a seagull with a pointed red beak, and the third was printed with a can of baked beans. 'April?' he asked again.

But instead of an answer, he heard a distant, desperate scream for help.

Chapter 32

'June!' shouted April. 'That's June, I know it. And she never asks for help; she must really be in trouble,' and her voice wobbled with anxiety. 'I'm going to make a run for it.'

'No, *don't*,' said Stuart urgently. 'It's not going to help June if you get into trouble as well. What if you fall down a hole? I wouldn't know who to rescue first, would I?'

'No, but . . .' He could hear that she was near tears. '*One* minute to solve it,' she said. 'I'll set my watch timer. OK? And if we've not solved it in one minute, I'm just going to guess.'

'OK.'

He looked at the paving stones again.

X. Gull. Beans.

'Beans, Gull, X,' he said, out loud.

'X is the Roman numeral for ten,' said April. 'Tony *Horten*?'

'Except it's not pronounced like that. All these clues have been about how the words *sound*, not how they're spelled.'

'Tin, then,' said April impatiently. 'The third one's a tin of beans. Tony Hor*tin*.'

'It's still not right.'

'Thirty seconds to go.'

'You pronounce it more like *turn*,' said Stuart. 'Tea Knee Tine E Tone Hee Haw Turn.'

'Turn?'

'Yes.'

'That's not a gull.'

'What?'

'That's not a picture of a gull. I did a summer holiday project on sea-birds when we went to Pembrokeshire last year. It's not a gull – their beaks look different. It's a *tern*!' And she was already off, jumping ahead, the minute timer on her wristwatch beeping, and Stuart hurried to catch up with her, galloping up the steps to the parapet. And from there, when he turned, he could see all four paths stretching back to the far wall. Two of them – the two that Stuart and April had completed – were no longer patterned, but had turned to solid paths of pure white flagstones. Halfway along one of the others was a dripping black blob.

'That's May!' shouted April, waving both arms. 'She must have fallen in that horrible bog. May!'

A wail of rage floated up from the black blob. 'I *said* . . . I *said* that it might be dangerous, and *nobody listened* – nobody *ever* listens to *meeeeee*.'

'And there's June,' said Stuart, pointing at a tiny figure in the far distance. 'She's not in trouble, she just hasn't got started yet. I'll go and get her, if you like.'

April nodded gratefully, and Stuart hurried away down June's path, happy to have avoided the task of escorting a smelly, furious May to safety.

Negotiating the path the other way round was harder than he'd imagined, involving a number of tricky leaps, and it wasn't until he had nearly reached June that he realized she was sitting with her eyes tightly shut and her fingers jammed in her ears, water pooling around her. She had obviously fallen into the icy water beneath the second flagstone.

'June!' he shouted from the paving stone with the picture of the teapot. 'It's me, Stuart.'

'Go away,' she said, removing one of her fingers. 'I'm having an extremely vivid dream.'

'No you're not.'

'I must be. It's the only possible explanation.'

'But how could I be in the same dream as you?'

'Because you're not actually Stuart, you're just a projection of my imagination. You probably represent a minor worry I'm having.'

'But—' He could see from her face that arguing was going to be a waste of time. 'OK,' he said, 'you're totally right, June, this is all a dream.'

'I knew it!' For the first time, she opened her eyes.

'And what I represent is' – he thought extremely hard – 'your minor worry about having to be in charge the whole time.'

'Yes, that is a worry,' she said, looking slightly pleased. 'My sisters don't understand what a responsibility it is.'

'So the thing about this dream is, you don't have to be in charge.'

'Don't I?'

'No. In this dream, you just have to listen to what I say, and do exactly what I do.'

'But—'

'With *no* arguing. Is that clear?'

She nodded slowly.

'So stand up,' he said, 'and follow me.'

Ordering a Kingley sister around was a new and enjoyable sensation, and they reached the end of the path with speedy efficiency. As they mounted the steps, Stuart turned and saw the jumbled pattern of June's path change, paving stone by paving stone, to an unbroken white, and then he hurried up to the parapet.

The other two triplets were still only halfway along May's path, and April was engaged in dragging her sister onto the alphabet stone. May had obviously almost missed the jump, and had accidentally kicked open the dank, dark entrance to the spiral staircase.

'This part of the dream shows exactly what happens when I'm *not* in charge,' remarked June, watching with interest.

Her sisters had nearly reached the steps when April paused and looked back.

'What's the matter?' called Stuart.

'I thought I heard something,' she shouted. 'Hang on a moment,' and she turned back along the path.

May stood there, paralysed.

'You're almost there,' said Stuart, coming down the steps towards her. 'Just jump onto the picture of the gull, and then onto the steps.'

'Yes, do what he says,' called June. 'He might look like Stuart, but he's actually a figment of my imagination, and therefore completely trustworthy.'

In the distance, April was kneeling, peering down the spiral staircase.

'Do I smell?' asked May, squelching up the steps and leaving a repulsive smudge on each one.

'No,' lied Stuart, trying to breathe through his mouth.

'I do. I smell like an outside *toilet*.'

And then April straightened up again, and Stuart realized that she was holding something brown and white with a briskly wagging tail.

'You got him!' he yelled, arms in the air.

'I got him!' repeated April. 'I heard little footsteps coming up the staircase and I knew it was him!' And she started back towards the steps, her arms firmly wrapped around Charlie.

'What's happening to the path?' asked May.

'What?'

'The path behind April.'

Stuart looked towards where she was pointing, and his blood seemed to freeze. The paving stones were turning white, one by one, as if a giant paintbrush were sweeping along the path, blanking the patterns, filling in the holes and cracks. 'Run!' he screamed at April, his voice scratchy with fear. '*Run!*'

She glanced behind her, gave a yelp of fear and began to hurry.

'Come on!' screamed May.

'This bit of the dream must represent a more major worry,' remarked June. 'Perhaps my upcoming Grade Two Piano exam.'

'Will you shut up about your stupid piano exam!' shouted May over her shoulder. 'Don't you get it? For once in your life, you're *wrong*. This isn't a dream, this is *real*.'

'Hurry!' shouted Stuart, his voice cracking, but April was only a few stones ahead of the paintbrush now, and her footsteps were uneven with panic. She managed the long jump from *Tone* to *Hee Haw*, but then stumbled, tried a desperate half-hop and landed squarely on the picture of the light bulb.

And stuck there, like a mouse trapped in glue.

'I can't lift my feet,' she shouted, struggling frantically. 'You'll have to help me.'

Stuart leaped forward, but May was even faster, knocking him aside as she thundered down the steps to save her sister, and he was just picking himself up again when June surged past, shouting, 'I can't work out the logic of this at all, but I'm coming, April! I'm coming to rescue you!' and treading heavily on Stuart's foot along the way.

So he was a few steps behind them when they reached the pathway, and could only shout in horror when the white tide engulfed first April and the dog, and then both her sisters, leaving nothing behind but blank stones and emptiness.

Chapter 33

'Come back!' Stuart yelled. '*Please!*' But no one answered. The lights in the huge room began to dim.

'April!' he called, his voice lost in the vastness. On the path ahead of him, a glowing letter 'I' flickered briefly on every paving stone, and then, with a neck-clicking jolt, Stuart found himself back in the shed again.

The door opened, and a man in overalls looked in.

'You still here?' he asked. 'I'm just locking up for the night, and Mr Kingley asked me to check round before I left. Where are the girls?'

'Gone,' said Stuart. He felt limp with shock, his voice a husk.

'OK, well, out you come.'

'Just a minute . . .' Desperately needing some time to think, he looked about for an excuse, and saw his own feet, one in a trainer, one in a filthy, slime-covered sock. 'My shoe,' he said. 'I've lost my shoe in here somewhere.'

The man shrugged. 'You've got two minutes while I go and get my stuff. After that you're out of here, shoe or no shoe.'

He left the door open and the early evening sun flooded in. Only one of Great-Uncle Tony's illusions seemed to reflect it back; the only illusion that hadn't been used yet – the Book of Peril, its dented satin surface glowing in the reddish light, the lettering on its door a fiery warning:

OPEN AT YOUR PERIL

And Stuart knew that the only possible route to getting the triplets back was through that door – a door that was damaged, a door that might lead to a world that was more dangerous than Great-Uncle Tony had ever intended.

You wanted to go on the last adventure on your own, he reminded himself grimly. *You wanted to be the only one to find that final clue. Well, you've got your wish.* It seemed so trivial now, all those worries about April finding the will first.

He only had a minute before the workman came back, and he hurried over to the Cabinet of Blood, feeling around between the sword hilts for the Magic Star, but his fingers found only an empty gap. He looked around wildly; it must have fallen onto the floor, but the floor was a mass of shadows and cracks – it could have rolled *anywhere*.

'Found it?' asked the man, returning.

'No, not yet.'

'Sorry, mate, you'll just have to go home in your sock. I'm sure the boss will let you in first thing on Monday to find it.' He was steering Stuart by the shoulder as he spoke, guiding him out into the yard.

'Monday?' echoed Stuart stupidly. 'But today's Friday. I can't wait two whole days.'

'You'll have to – we're closed all weekend. And I'd

hop across here if I was you – you don't want to get a nail through that foot, do you?' He was locking the shed door, pocketing the key, pointing to the exit, and Stuart was left with no choice but to accompany him (hopping) across the yard and out. The gates clanged shut, and the man bolted and padlocked them and then strode away whistling, and Stuart was left standing alone, staring hopelessly up at the high wall that ran around the yard, knowing only that he had to get back in. Somehow.

'Ladder,' he said out loud. 'I need a ladder,' and then pictured himself trying to scale the wall in full view of passers-by. Not that there were many – across the road from the yard there was only an empty shop, a piece of waste ground and a large locked garage with EL-ECTRIC painted on the doors. Even so, it would be best to wait until dark before starting.

Torch, he thought. *Screwdriver. Shoe. Some kind of brilliant story to explain to my father why I have to go out for the entire evening (and possibly half the night as well).*

*

He still hadn't thought of one when he turned the corner into Beech Road, and his worries weren't helped by the fact that the first person he saw was Mrs Kingley, the triplets' mother. She was standing on the front step of her house, peering along the road, and she smiled in relief when she saw Stuart.

'Aha, here's someone who can tell me when those girls are getting back.'

She waited expectantly, and Stuart summoned up all his acting powers and replied, 'Oh, I don't think they'll be long – they were a bit busy when I saw them last,' and then limped quickly towards his house before she could ask him anything more.

His father was in the kitchen, chopping beetroot and frowning at a recipe book, opened at a page entitled 'Multi-Vitamin Bake'. A radio programme about the history of encyclopaedias was on in the background.

'Dad,' said Stuart hurriedly, 'I'm not being rude or anything, and I'm sure that the Vitamin Bake would be really delicious, but if it's OK with you, I've got to dash out again and I wondered if I could just have a sandwich. A healthy one, obviously. It's only that I've got to go and … and …' His imagination failed him, and he found himself (sort of) telling the truth. 'I've got to go and get the triplets. They're lost in a book.'

His father smiled nostalgically. 'Ah yes, how well I know that feeling. How many times have I found myself wandering in a pathless thicket of words … Beetroot sandwich?' he added. 'Or I could offer curly kale, spinach or shiitake mushroom.'

There was a pause.

'Cheese?' suggested his father.

'Yes please.'

'And this post-prandial book-extraction exped-ition – can you assure me you'll be safely with the Kingley sorority throughout?'

Stuart swallowed. 'They're waiting for me and I won't come back without them, I promise, Dad. I absolutely promise.'

His father nodded, satisfied. 'Before I forget, you've just missed an unexpected maternal telephonic communication. However, I assured your mother that your health was fully restored, which I hope was an accurate report?'

'Yup,' said Stuart, grabbing his sandwich and taking a large bite. 'Thanks, Dad. I've just got to get something before I go out again.'

He headed for the hall and rummaged around in the cupboard under the stairs. The only torch he could find was a miniature key-ring in the shape of the Eiffel Tower, and the only screwdriver was bright pink and out of a cracker. The ladder was just a kitchen stool with a couple of steps attached – mainly useful for getting jars of pickled onions out of high cupboards – but it was better than nothing, and he was about to hurry out with it through the front door when the phone rang.

'Hello?' he said, snatching up the receiver, expecting to hear his mother.

There was a rattle of static on the line.

'Hello?' he repeated.

'*Stuart.*'

That voice again; a vigorous rasp, old yet full of life.

'Miss Edie,' said Stuart.

Chapter 34

'*Made any progress?*'

'A bit.'

'*Only I've just recalled something else my gramma told me about the will – it jumped into my mind when I was sitting thinking about her. She was a stern lady as well as a smart one, and when she talked, you listened. You listening now?*' she added sharply, almost as if she could see that Stuart was distractedly hopping from foot to foot.

'I don't have much time,' he said. 'Something's happened.'

'*You've got a problem?*'

'Yes, a huge problem and I've got to sort it out.'

'*Don't forget what I told you. If you're rich enough, then problems just melt away.*'

'It's not that sort of problem. I could have fifty billion pounds and it wouldn't solve this one. I've got to go.'

'*No, you've got to stay and listen.*' Her voice was suddenly fierce, and Stuart felt as if he'd been poked with a skewer. '*I told you that my gramma said Tony Horten's will was well hidden – he told her that himself – but what I've recalled now is this: she said you should use the male to find it. The male. Does that help you any?*'

'No.'

'*You sure? You haven't put your mind to it for more than a single second. Take some time and see if you can figure it out.*'

'Don't you understand?' Stuart was almost shouting with exasperation. 'I don't have *time* to worry about the will – I'm trying to find something that's loads more important than a piece of paper. I'm trying to find my *friends.*'

There was a short, sharp pause.

'*Well now,*' said Miss Edie coldly, '*my gramma always said that you were nothing but trouble and sass, and I can see now that she was—*'

There was another burst of static on the line, and then nothing but an echoey hiss. Stuart stared at the receiver; his mouth was dry and he felt as if someone had just dropped an ice-cube down his back.

'Your grandma never met me,' he whispered into the silence. 'She died years before I was born.'

The kitchen stool was awkward and surprisingly heavy to carry, and it was dusk by the time Stuart arrived back at the yard. A woman was walking her dog along the road, but once she'd gone past there was no one else to be seen. Stuart climbed onto the stool. Stretching to his full height, he was still nowhere near the top of the wall, and he could now see that there were pieces of glass embedded in the mortar at the top. He got down again, went over to the double gates and fingered the enormous padlock. He took out the elf-sized screwdriver, compared it to the size of the screws in the gate hinges, and put it back in his pocket again. It was too small. *He* was too small. In frustration, he kicked at the base of the gates and heard the hollow boom of metal. He kicked at it again, and missed, his foot slipping into the gap between the gates and the ground.

'Ow,' said Stuart, rubbing his ankle. He knelt down to look. The road surface beneath the gates was heavily rutted and potholed, and near the centre was a gap that was just possibly large enough for a small, thin person to wriggle through.

Just possibly.

Night was falling rapidly now. The street was still empty, but from the EL-ECTRIC garage opposite, a small yellow diamond of light shone through the only window. Odd sounds of hammering came from within.

Stuart lay down and started to inch forward, head first. The ground was rough beneath his cheek, and the lower edge of the gate scraped through his hair like a toothless comb. He wriggled forward a little further, and something tiny and painful and pointy dug into his cheek – a screw or a stone chip, perhaps – and he flinched and felt his opposite ear fold agonizingly beneath the gate . . . and that was it: he was stuck fast, panic bubbling through his limbs.

His legs flailed helplessly across the pavement, and he must have cried out because he suddenly heard the noise of the garage door opening. He held his breath.

'Hullo?' called a man's voice that seemed somehow familiar. 'Anyone in trouble?'

Stuart kept absolutely still.

'Close the door!' called another voice urgently – a woman this time. 'You'll let Gerald out!'

'Oh. Sorry.'

Across the road, the door scraped shut again, and Stuart took a breath. He reached up with one hand and tried to unfold his ear, and he had almost managed it when he felt something climb onto his ankle.

Something small, with claws and whiskers and wiry fur; it paused for a split second and then shot up the leg of Stuart's jeans.

Stuart yelled.

Chapter 35

And yelled.

The garage door opened again, more hurriedly this time, and loud footsteps crossed towards him. 'Are you OK?' asked the vaguely familiar voice.

'There's a rat!' screamed Stuart, head still stuck under the gate, one hand clutching the knee of his jeans to stop the creature going any further. 'There's a rat up my trouser leg.'

'Is that *Stuart*?' asked the man incredulously.

'Get it out of there.'

'Stuart *Horten*?'

'*Yes*.'

'It's Clifford!'

'It's a *rat*!'

'No it's not,' said the woman's voice reassuringly.

'It's a guinea pig. He ran out when the door opened earlier. I'll catch him, and if Clifford fetches my car-jack from the garage I'll be able to raise the gate and get you out of there.'

It was only a minute or two before Stuart was sitting on an upturned crate in the garage, ear throbbing, biscuit in hand, guinea pig on lap.

'He's called Gerald after my father,' said Clifford. 'They've both got ginger eyebrows, you see. Elaine and I were just practising the guinea-pig disappearing act for our next performance – I really feel we're starting to improve. The lighting's still a great deal better than the trick, of course . . .'

'Have another biscuit,' said the woman, Elaine. She was the small, pale-faced electrician who'd come to see Clifford's first show, and this was obviously her workshop. It was highly organized – tools hanging on the walls, equipment neatly marshalled. In the centre of the room stood Mysterioso the Magician's trolley, no longer looking shabby and makeshift, but glimmering with myriad tiny lights.

'I don't really have time,' replied Stuart. 'I have to get into Mr Kingley's yard. Somehow.'

'Why?'

And because it was Clifford who asked the question – Clifford who had seen *real* magic (who had actually been there, just inches away, when Stuart and the mayoress, Jeannie Carr, had disappeared into the Well of Wishes, dissolving into the past like a splash of water into a pond) – Stuart found that he was able to tell him everything.

Afterwards, there was a long silence.

Clifford's eyes were shining. 'Wonderful things,' he said. 'More wonderful than I realized. No wonder Jeannie was so desperate to get her hands on them.'

'Wonderful,' agreed Stuart, 'but dangerous too.'

'Of course we'll help you get into the yard, won't we?' said Clifford, looking over at Elaine.

She nodded, her expression entranced. 'And would you like us to come with you into the Book of Peril?' she asked.

'No,' said Stuart firmly. 'There'd be too many people for me to keep track of. What if you got lost as well?'

Elaine stood up. 'Just give me a minute or two to prepare,' she said.

Quickly and efficiently she filled a tool-bag, folded a square rubber mat – 'to get us over the glass' – and slung a lightweight set of ladders over her shoulder. 'Ready,' she said.

Clifford nudged Stuart. '*She's absolutely marvellous, isn't she?*' he whispered.

Elaine blushed. 'Let's get going,' she said.

With Elaine organizing things, they were up and over the wall within five minutes, and into the shed in another three.

'The Magic Star...' said Stuart, peering at the floor.

'For that, I have a wand.' Elaine took what looked like a slender steel aerial out of her bag, extended it like a telescope, and waved it across the floor.

There was a series of clinks, and when she lifted it into the beam of Stuart's torch, it was encrusted with small screws and nails. Right at the tip was the single remaining bar of the Magic Star.

'Not magic but magnetic,' said Elaine, grinning.

Stuart took the star. In the torchlight, the dented cover of the Book of Peril was like the entrance to a dark passageway, the silvery letters – OPEN AT YOUR PERIL – floating in the air. Stuart tugged on the handle and the door swung wide, though it groaned as it opened, as if the dent had affected the hinges.

'Where does the star go?' asked Clifford.

By way of reply, Stuart crouched down and prised open the secret compartment where he and April had found Great-Uncle Tony's message. April was the one who had spotted a single groove in the floor of the compartment, and at the time Stuart hadn't known what it was for.

Now he did.

He took a breath to steady his nerves. His fingers were clenched around the star, but he could feel them trembling.

'How long will you be?' asked Clifford.

'As long as it takes me to find the Kingleys and bring them back,' said Stuart. 'It might be hours and hours.'

'We'll wait, don't worry. And Stuart . . . ?'

'Yes?'

'Have you changed your mind? Would you like us to come along?'

Stuart couldn't trust himself to speak, in case another 'yes' slipped out. His skin prickled with fear, and he desperately wanted company, but he knew that two extra people might make things even more complicated, just as they had in the Cabinet of Blood. So instead of speaking, he smiled, shook his head, and quickly and carefully fitted the last spoke of the Magic Star into the Book of Peril.

And gasped.

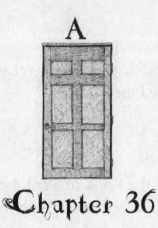

Chapter 36

He was in his own kitchen.

It was broad daylight.

His mum was standing by the cooker with her back to him, while through the window Stuart could see his father sitting in a deckchair on the lawn, staring into space, while an eager Charlie ran in tight circles around him. The Kingley triplets were in their own garden, standing in a row with their chins resting on the fence, and one of them spotted Stuart in the kitchen window and gave a frantic wave.

'April!' shouted Stuart joyfully, amazed at how simple the rescue was going to be.

He turned to wrench open the back door, and stopped short. Right next to the door was a tall shimmering black panel, and across it, in silver lettering, floated the words:

OPEN AT YOUR PERIL

He was *inside* the Book of Peril, he realized, and the shimmering black panel (with its central dent) was the way out, and when he pressed his face to its surface he could dimly see the interior of the shed, as if viewed through inky water. Clifford and Elaine were standing together, his arm round her shoulders, waiting for him. All Stuart had to do was go out into the garden, fetch Charlie and the triplets, and take them back through this dark doorway into the shed and it would all be over.

He reached for the handle of the back door.

'Stuart,' said his mother, 'your nuggets and fries are ready.'

Stuart's hand froze.

Slowly, slowly, he turned towards his mother. She was holding a plate out towards him. On it was a vast stack of chicken nuggets, a hillock of chips and a lake of tomato ketchup. Next to the lake was a very large pinch of salt.

'More salt?' asked his mother.

'No thanks,' said Stuart hoarsely.

He took the plate and walked like a zombie to the table. Through the window he could see the triplets, still watching him but beginning to look impatient now.

'Stuart!' called April. 'Hurry up! We want to get out of here!'

Still standing, he looked down at his plate again. A slick of grease was pooling around the chips.

'Eat up. There's treacle tart with condensed milk for pudding,' said his mother, 'and you still haven't eaten that stick of rock that your uncle sent you.'

'Is there an apple or something?' asked Stuart.

His mother shook her head. 'I keep forgetting to buy fruit.'

Stuart set the plate down.

This woman in the kitchen looked like his mother, but she wasn't. His mother never added salt to anything. His mother regarded chicken nuggets as a sort of slow-acting poison, and puddings as an opportunity for eating fruit. His mother would rather run out of *air* than apples.

He edged away from the table, wondering what he should do. Everything had seemed easy and obvious, but now he felt as if the ground was shuddering under him. He needed to put this right.

'Cola with that?' asked the woman, going to the fridge.

'*Don't rush,*' Stuart muttered to himself. '*Work it out. Think.*'

He looked around carefully. Everything looked normal – the roller blind that drooped on one side, the calendar with views of Great Libraries of the World, the photograph of Stuart and his parents in the Lake District. And then he spotted something strange and new on the door that led to the living room: the letter A, half visible, glimmering like a snail trail.

'Just got to get something,' he said, then slipped over to the door and opened it.

And found himself in the kitchen again, his mother at the stove.

He caught his breath and whirled round.

As before, the Book of Peril stood next to the back door. Through the kitchen window, he could see the triplets lined up against the fence, his father sitting in the deckchair and Charlie sniffing along the edge of the lawn.

'Lunch, Stuart,' said his mother. 'Pea and mint soup.'

'Thanks.'

'I'm going into work this afternoon. Can you let Dad know his food's ready?'

'OK.' He slipped out of the back door.

'Stuart!' shouted April. 'At last! Shall we climb over? Stuart? *Stuart!*'

But Stuart didn't answer. He was too busy staring, aghast, at his father, who had got out of the deckchair and was doing a series of press-ups on the grass.

'Shall we climb over the *fence?*' repeated April impatiently.

His father began to do the press-ups one-armed.

'No,' said Stuart, struggling to think. It was

somehow even more frightening to feel lost in his own home than it was in a trackless desert or a giant maze. 'Not this fence. Maybe the next one. I think – I think I have to choose the right life. And the right letter.'

He ran back indoors.

The letter B glimmered on the living-room door. Steeling himself for what might come next, he went through, and found himself in the kitchen again.

This time his father was cooking, peering anxiously at a recipe book. The page had a photograph of an artichoke.

'Where's Mum?' asked Stuart.

'Dunno,' said his dad. 'I think she said was going to get her nails done or something.'

Stuart went straight over to the living-room door.

The letter C.

This time the kitchen was empty, apart from Charlie curled up in a basket, but it smelled wonderfully of roast dinner. The garden was empty too, and there was no one standing by the fence.

'Hello?' called Stuart cautiously. 'Anyone at home?'

All was quiet. He waited for a moment or two, savouring the smell, and then took an apple from a bowl piled high with them. Above the fruit bowl, on the wall, was the photo of Stuart and his parents. He glanced at it, and dropped the apple. It fell with a dull thud and rolled across the kitchen floor.

There stood Stuart's father, his glasses spotted with rain, his mother, her hair blown into a thistle-shape by the wind, and Stuart, his nose bright red from the cold. And next to Stuart stood someone else – a boy, grinning. A boy who was a few centimetres shorter than Stuart, but who was otherwise his double.

In *this* world he had a brother.

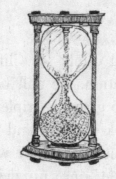

Chapter 37

Stuart didn't know how long he stood staring at the picture – only that he was jerked from his thoughts by a glassy crack. It came from the direction of the Book of Peril.

He hurried over and saw with a chill that the rippling darkness was now marred by a whitish circle around the dent. The surface there had paled and thickened, and he could no longer see through it. And – most worryingly – just as he reached out to touch it, there was another *crack!* and the opacity spread further, like ice forming on a pond.

His breathing quickened. What if the door stopped working? What would it mean? Might he be stuck for eternity in an empty kitchen?

He gave the door a tentative push, and it moved

slightly; he could dimly see Clifford and Elaine tense in anticipation. He still had a little time, then – enough to grab the triplets and dive back through the Book of Peril, and who cared if he got the letter clue completely wrong and never solved Great-Uncle Tony's puzzle? Getting back to the real world with them was the only important thing.

He hurried outside. There was still no sign of the triplets, so he shouted their names over the fence. The windows of their house looked blankly back at him. He jumped up and managed to glimpse their garden; it seemed to be weedier than he remembered, and Mr Kingley had obviously taken the barbecue indoors.

He took a huge breath and yelled April's name as loudly as he could, and to his relief he heard the Kingleys' back door open. Footsteps approached.

'Hello?' said a young man in a suit, frowning over the fence.

'Where are the Kingleys?' demanded Stuart.

'In Cornwall, I believe,' said the man. 'They moved there a couple of months ago. Which is why I'm now showing Mr and Mrs Lee around this well-maintained three-bedroom property in a tree-lined cul-de-sac.' He flashed a smile at a severe-looking elderly couple who had followed him out to the garden. 'They're looking for a *quiet* retirement residence,' he added pointedly.

Stuart didn't wait to hear any more. He hurtled straight back into the kitchen, and through the living-room door.

Letter D.

And the triplets were there, sitting in front of him at the kitchen table.

Knitting.

'Oh, hello, Stuart,' said June, smiling warmly at him, the dog lolling asleep on her lap. 'Lovely to see you – look what your mum's been teaching us. April's already made a doll's bonnet.'

'Isn't it lovely?' asked April in a soppy voice, waving something pink at him.

'We've got to go,' said Stuart brusquely, trying to ignore the awful weirdness of a world in which his mother could knit bonnets. 'Come on.'

'Not until I've learned how to make matching

bootees. Your mum's just gone to find some more wool.'

'We've got to *go*,' said Stuart, grabbing April's hand. She pulled away and gave a scream.

'What?' asked Stuart, confused. A length of pink wool was dangling from his fingers.

'You've *unravelled* it!' wailed April. 'That took me ages and ages, and now you've *ruined* it. I'm not going anywhere till it's all knitted again.'

'WE HAVEN'T GOT TIME FOR THAT!' shouted Stuart, so tense that he felt as if he might snap in half. He could see the crust of whiteness spreading across the dark panel of the door.

April burst into tears. 'He *shouted* at me,' she sobbed. 'I'm going *home*.' She flounced past Stuart and out of the back door.

'Now look what you've done,' said May reproachfully, going after her. 'You know how sensitive she is. It'll take hours and hours to talk her into coming back . . . Come on, June,' she added commandingly, and June scuttled after her, followed by Charlie.

The back door slammed.

Stuart heard himself give a despairing moan. He

looked at the Book of Peril, and saw the darkness being leached out of it, and he started to run after the triplets, and then changed his mind and plunged instead through the living-room door.

Letter E.

'Salutations,' said his father, sitting at the table with a pad of paper. 'Your mother will be home from her quotidian microscopic investigations in approximately—'

'Sorry, I'm in a hurry,' gabbled Stuart, running straight out into the garden. Which was somehow different, though he didn't have time to work out how, or why. He looked over the fence and saw the triplets sitting on their lawn, playing with Charlie, and he bellowed hoarsely to them, panic straining his voice.

'Hurrah!' shouted April, leaping to her feet. 'I knew you'd come,' and she hauled a garden chair across to the fence, and was over it in seconds, Charlie in her arms, her sisters hurriedly following.

'Come on,' said Stuart. 'Come on come on come on come on come on come *on*.'

'Would your visitors care for inter-prandial ingestion of—'

'No time, Dad,' said Stuart, hurling himself towards the Book of Peril. It looked like the top of an iced cake now, only a tiny section of the darkness visible around the edges. He gave it a shove and it buckled rather than opened, the top and the bottom curling in towards each other. He shoved again, and a crack opened on one side; he urged April and Charlie through, and then June, and then a wide-eyed May, and with one final look back at a kitchen that didn't look quite the same as usual, Stuart leaped through himself.

There was a noise like a giant light bulb breaking, a whoosh of air, and he fell into darkness onto a pile of shouting bodies, Charlie yapping, dust everywhere, clouds of it, gritty and stinging.

A torch flashed on, and then another.

'That was quick,' said Clifford.

'What?' asked Stuart, coughing, scooping up the dog before he could be trodden on.

'Less than half a minute. The door sort of twitched after twelve seconds and then disintegrated at twenty-eight.'

Stuart turned and looked at the gaping hole

where the door had been. The dust hung in the air like icing sugar, and through it he could just see the socket where the final spoke of the Magic Star had fitted. It was empty now.

'It might have been twenty-eight seconds for you, Stuart, but we were away for *ages*,' grumbled May, getting to her feet. 'When we went back to unglue April from that path, everything got sort of fuzzy, and then we found ourselves in our house – but it wasn't really our house at all, it was like a stage set. There was no upstairs, the front garden was just mist, and there was nothing on the telly except static. We were just waiting and waiting and waiting, and it was all because no one listened to me when I said it would be dangerous, and then it *was*, and no one listened to me when I said we'd get stuck there, and then we *did*! Is it the same day, even?'

Stuart nodded.

'Well, thank goodness for that!'

'It was boring and weird and horrid,' added April quietly. 'But I knew you'd come and get us. Thank you.'

'Yes, thanks, Stuart,' said May, giving him a deeply embarrassing hug.

'That's all right,' he said gruffly, 'and I couldn't have done it without help.' He gestured to Clifford and Elaine.

'We'd better get you all out of here,' said Elaine. 'Before we get caught.'

'And before our mum does her nut,' added April. She held out a hand to help up June, who was still sitting on the floor.

'I've had the oddest dream,' she said.

'Oh, for *goodness' sake*,' screeched May, 'it was *not* a dream. When are you *ever* going to admit it?'

April rolled her eyes at Stuart. '*It's been like this the whole time*,' she whispered. '*I've had to be incredibly tolerant and patient, and then when she . . .*' She paused and frowned.

'What?' asked Stuart.

She looked at him, tilting her head. 'You look different,' she said. 'Apart from being covered in dust, I mean.'

'What sort of different?'

'Older.'

'What?'

'No, not older . . .' She paused, and her eyes widened. 'Taller.'

'*What?*'

'Taller. A bit, anyway.'

'Come on, everybody,' said Elaine firmly. 'Out. And let's be as quiet as cats.'

Stuart, light-headed with shock, was scarcely aware of the tiptoed journey across the yard, the scurry over the ladder, the rushed farewells to Elaine and Clifford, the jog through the darkened town, with Charlie drooping tiredly in his arms.

What April said couldn't be true, could it? And yet . . . in the Book of Peril, when he had dashed outside for the last time, he had spotted the triplets in their garden. Which meant that *he had been able to see over the fence*. Without jumping. Without standing on a box. And maybe the kitchen in that world had looked different, not because of anything in it, but because he'd suddenly been viewing it *from a different height*. And maybe the wrong factor in that particular world hadn't been his dad or his mum, or even the triplets – it had been *him*.

'There's Mum,' said April rather nervously, jerking Stuart out of his thoughts. They had reached Beech Road, and Mrs Kingley was standing on the front doorstep, her arms folded. She said nothing at all as they approached, but simply pointed inside.

'*Bye*,' mouthed April to Stuart. '*See you tomorrow*.'

He watched them file silently into their house. The front door clicked shut, there was a pause – and then the sound of Mrs Kingley shouting. Stuart scuttled off to his own front door, and bent his knees slightly before ringing the bell. Just in case his father spotted anything different.

But it was his mother who answered the door.

'Surprise!' she said. 'I was actually phoning from the airport, but I didn't—' She stopped speaking and stared at him.

'You've *grown*,' she said. 'And you've found a dog.'

'I know,' replied Stuart, his voice coming out a bit wobbly. 'Surprise!'

hello

❧Chapter 38

It was two days later, and Stuart was hanging around in the back garden, waiting for April to appear.

Charlie was also in the garden. Apart from eating, the little dog's main occupation was following Stuart around, gazing up at him adoringly – so adoringly that even Stuart's mother (who wasn't particularly keen on pets) had agreed to keep him for the time being.

'Until we can find the *original* owner,' she'd insisted, and Stuart had happily gone along with that condition. At the present moment Charlie was resting his head on Stuart's right shoe and nibbling the shoe-lace.

'Good dog,' said Stuart. The stump of tail wagged keenly.

Stuart looked at his watch. Since their return, April and her sisters had been confined to the house as a punishment for staying out late without permission, and April had communicated with Stuart by means of written messages held up to the window of her bedroom.

MY MUM SAYS WE ARE NEVER ALLOWED OUT AGAIN UNTIL WE ARE 18.

had been the first one, followed – a few hours later – by:

SHE'S NOW REDUCED IT TO A WEEK, BUT WE HAVE TO WORK FOR OUR FREEDOM.

Stuart had gone and got paper of his own, and had written the word HOW? and held it up to her.

UNECCESARY HOMEWORK, HOUSEWORK AND PIANO PRACTICE.

had been the answer.

ANYTHING I CAN DO? asked Stuart.

YES. TELL ME WHAT LETTER CLUE YOU
GOT OUT OF THE BOOK OF PERIL.

E, wrote Stuart in reply.

On the second morning, a grinning April had
brandished a sign reading:

SENTENCE REDUCED ON ACCOUNT OF
ME PLAYING 'DANCE OF THE SHEPHERD
GIRLS' 323 TIMES IN A ROW, WHICH
MUM SAID WAS DRIVING HER TOTALLY
MAD. OUT AT 11 O'CLOCK.

It was five to eleven now.

Stuart looked at the triplets' garden, still
marvelling that he could actually see over the fence;
he'd grown nearly four centimetres – which meant
that although he was still short for his age, for the
time being he was only a *bit* short. 'A sudden growth
spurt,' his mother had decided, after measuring
him. 'Unusual but not unprecedented. I expect it

was the combination of the heat stress you endured and Dad's splendidly healthy cooking. I've actually read a recent paper about the positive effects of spinach and kale on human bone growth – I think we should definitely keep them on the menu.'

Which meant that Stuart wasn't particularly looking forward to the sort of meals he'd be getting from now on.

The Kingleys' back door opened and one of the triplets came out.

'Hi, June,' said Stuart.

She looked surprised, and slightly gratified that he'd identified her correctly. 'April says to tell you that she's just coming. She's been working on something to show you. And I wanted to say thank you for coming to get us. I've realized now that it wasn't a dream.'

'Oh, right,' said Stuart, impressed. He hadn't realized that June *ever* changed her mind.

'No, it wasn't a dream,' she continued, 'it was an extremely vivid hallucination probably brought on by inhaling fumes from the old-fashioned lead-based paint your great-uncle used in the illusions.'

'Oh.' He couldn't be bothered to argue. 'OK.'

'But you snapped us out of it and got us home. So thanks.'

She disappeared back into the house, and after a moment April came out. Stuart felt ridiculously pleased to see her; they'd only known each other for just over a month, but he felt as if they'd been friends for years and years and years. She grinned back at him over the fence and then held up a piece of paper for him to see.

THE COMPLETED CLUES:

The Pharaoh's Pyramid	S
The Arch of Mirrors	W
The Fan of Fantasticality	O
The Reappearing Rose Bower	T
The Cabinet of Blood	I
The Book of Peril	E

'I've been working and working on this,' she said. 'I tried every anagram possible and then gave up on that idea, and then I thought that they might be initials for something. SWOT could stand for *South West Of The.*'

'South West Of The what?' asked Stuart.

'That's the trouble – I could only think of stupid things. Icelandic Egg. Idiotic Exhibition.'

'Irish Elephant,' suggested Stuart.

'So *then* I wondered if it was a number thing – you know, S is the nineteenth letter of the alphabet, and W is the twenty-third, and so on, so I added up all the numbers and got two hundred and twenty-five. Does that seem a significant number to you at all?'

Stuart shook his head.

'Nor me,' said April. 'So then I read a code book that June got for Christmas, and there's hundreds of ways to write codes: you can substitute one letter for another, or decide to move them so many places up or down the alphabet, or swap them round, or count backwards, and I tried loads and loads and loads of them – I mean, I didn't have anything else to do apart from practise "Dance of the Shepherd Girls" – and in the end I came to a conclusion.'

'What?' asked Stuart.

'That it's not a code. Because in the end, all a code would give you is a six-letter word, and that wouldn't be enough of a clue. Even if it was *inside* or *behind* or *mirror* or *swivel*. I mean, we've pretty much explored every nook and cranny of those illusions and we haven't found the will, have we? It must be hidden somewhere complicated and hard to find, and one word just isn't going to give us the answer.'

She was probably right, Stuart thought – she generally was, about most things. But there was something else nagging at the back of his mind.

'I had another phone call,' he said, 'from Miss Edie. When you were trapped with your sisters. I didn't have time to talk to her properly, but she said she'd remembered a couple of things that might help with the search.'

'What?'

'She said that her grandma told her that the will was well hidden, but that we should use the male to find it.'

'The *male*?'

'Yes.'

'What, as in *man*? Does that mean only *you* can find it, and not *me*? Or does she mean that only a grown-up can get it?'

'I don't know. And she said something else – something really, *really* odd. She said that her grandma hadn't liked me much.'

'Her grandma who died eighty years ago?'

'That's the one.'

'How could she ever have met you?'

'I don't know.'

'Well, what *do* you know about her?'

'That she was a very clever businesswoman. She came to Canada from England. And she said that I was nothing but trouble.'

Stuart and April looked at each other across the top of the fence – stared at each other really hard – and the same idea came to them simultaneously, so that they both gave a little hop, as if electrocuted, and spoke the two syllables at the same time.

'*Jeannie!*'

Chapter 39

Jeannie Carr, the mayoress of Beeton, was Miss Edie's grandmother!

Jeannie Carr, who had been so desperate to find Great-Uncle Tony's workshop that she had threatened and bribed and followed Stuart, and had finally been catapulted back into Victorian England by the Well of Wishes – a Victorian England that had also contained Great-Uncle Tony, who had gone back in search of his fiancée. That's where Jeannie had found out about the hidden will.

'She never stopped wanting to get the tricks,' said April, eyes wide, 'her whole life long!'

Stuart thought about the last time he'd seen Jeannie, standing furious and aghast on the stage of a Victorian theatre, doomed to remain in the past.

A tiny part of him felt slightly relieved that she had not only survived being flung back into history but had actually flourished – had emigrated and founded a family and a fortune. *She left England with ten pounds in her pocket and a headful of ideas,* Miss Edie had said, *and she set up a factory in Canada and made more money than you would ever believe* . . .

'So did Miss Edie tell you how much she was prepared to pay for the tricks?' asked April.

Stuart hesitated before answering. April and he had been through so much together; he felt that he owed her the truth.

'Enough to make me very, very rich. Enough for limousines and club class on aeroplanes and months in Disneyland.'

'Oh,' said April, for once lost for words. 'Wow. I didn't realize.'

A silence fell between them, broken only by Charlie growling at Stuart's shoe-lace.

'I expect you'd move house, then,' said April. 'To somewhere bigger. With a swimming pool and stuff.'

'Well,' said Stuart awkwardly, 'it's too early to say. And I haven't even found the will yet, have I? And I can't really ask Elaine to keep breaking into your dad's yard, and I don't suppose he'll let us just walk in, will he?'

'No.' April smiled ruefully. 'He says that's the last time he'll ever do us a favour, *ever*. He's keeping the key until the museum's got room for the illusions again.'

'And when's that going to be?'

'When the Roman Beeton exhibition opens on Saturday. Rod Felton rang Dad to say he was going to try and squeeze them into the storeroom, since so many people had signed the *Beech Road Guardian*'s petition.' She bridled at Stuart's amazed expression. 'I know you don't think much of our newspaper,' she said, rather huffily, 'but it's actually read by people as far away as Chestnut Avenue. And May sold the photo of Rod Felton crashing into that reporter to a national newspaper for a two-figure sum. Eleven pounds, to be exact.'

'So you're going to carry on writing for it?'

'Of course. I'll be reviewing the exhibition. And while we're there we should get a chance to look at the tricks again – and maybe by then we'll have worked out what the clues mean.'

In the days that followed, Stuart was kept occupied with quite ordinary things – buying PE kit and uniform for his new school, and visiting his grandparents – but the ordinary things felt extraordinary, since the PE kit was two sizes larger than he'd needed at the beginning of the summer, and his grandparents kept going on and on about how much he'd shot up. And all the while, the letters SWOTIE seemed to rattle around inside his head, like marbles in a tin.

On the day before the opening he heard a familiar voice from the living room, and he hurried through to look at the TV.

'And that's *all* from *Midlands at Midday*,' announced Rowena Allsopp, smiling toothily. 'Tomorrow I'm off to the *museum* in the historic town of *Beeton* to sign copies of my autobiography, *Rowena's Way*, and also to open two brand-new exhi*bitions*.'

'And what are those exhibitions about, Rowena?' asked the man in the suit sitting next to her.

'One of them is a *fascinating* display of the *outfits* I've worn over the years on this *very* programme, and the other one's about, er, history or something. So see you *tomorrow*!' She waved and then pretended to tidy up her papers.

'Yup,' said Stuart to the television. 'See you tomorrow.'

Chapter 40

There was a surprisingly large crowd waiting outside the museum the next day, and quite a lot of dissatisfied muttering when Stuart and April and Stuart's father went straight to the head of the queue and were let in by the receptionist.

'How come you're getting in early?' asked one man, who was holding a black-and-gold autograph book and wearing a badge with a smiling picture of Rowena Allsopp on it.

'I'm a reporter,' said April, holding up her notebook.

'I'm a mini curator,' said Stuart, pointing to his badge.

'I'm merely the possessor of an ardent and enduring curiosity anent the pre-Christian antecedents of contemporary Midland conurbations,' said Stuart's father.

'Oh,' said the Rowena fan. 'Fair enough.'

Rod Felton met them in the foyer. He was wearing a mustard-coloured tweed suit and a tie covered in Roman numerals, and he was practically dancing with excitement. 'Just wait till you see the centrepiece,' he said. 'We have a full-sized ballista, and a replica apodyterium with adjoining balneum with niches for subligaculae!'

'A replica what?' asked April, scribbling frantically.

'And we have a gastraphetes!'

'A gastraphetes?' gasped Stuart's father, apparently awestruck.

'A replica *what*?' repeated April patiently.

'And an oxybeles!'

'An oxybeles?'

'Excuse me,' said Stuart. 'Do you think I could possibly see where you've put my great-uncle's tricks?'

It took a moment or two for Rod Felton to re-focus his attention, and then he waved his arm vaguely towards a door labelled STAFF ONLY. 'Down there,' he said. 'They've only just arrived so I've not seen them yet.'

'An oxybeles!' repeated Stuart's father dreamily.

'*I'll be with you in five minutes*,' mouthed April. Stuart nodded and slipped through the door.

A flight of concrete steps led down to a basement, lit by a skylight that ran the length of the room. At first glance it looked like an overcrowded junk shop. A large stuffed antelope stood at the bottom of the stairs next to a faded mummy case. There were suits of armour and leather buckets, gas masks, spinning wheels, a red motorbike and a black penny-farthing. There was even the giant fake carthorse that only a few weeks before had been accidentally knocked over and broken. By Stuart. Twice. And crammed into a far corner, right next to the freight lift, were Great-Uncle Tony's illusions.

They were huddled together like nervous visitors, and Stuart approached them slowly, and with growing dismay.

Two trips in a builder's van had chipped and dented them. Paint had flaked, wires were bent, metallic edges curled or blunted. The Pharaoh's Pyramid had a broken door, the Book of Peril had no door at all, the swords in the Cabinet of Blood were twisted, the silver stems of the Reappearing Rose Bower looked wild and wind-blown, the Fan of Fantasticality drooped on one side, and the Arch of Mirrors was blotched with black patches where mirrors had dropped off or smashed. They sat dully in the bright morning light, like unloved tin toys.

Stuart felt heavy with guilt; he had found the workshop and used up all the magic, but he had failed to look after its contents. They needed care and skill and love and knowledge and time.

'Stuart!' It was April, calling over the banister. 'The opening ceremony's about to start. Have you found anything?'

He shook his head and followed her up the stairs. 'I don't know where to begin,' he said as they hurried along the corridor.

'We're missing something obvious,' said April, frowning. 'I just *know* we are.'

They emerged into the large central room of the museum.

One end was dominated by the Roman catapult (or *ballista*, as Rod Felton insisted on calling it). It looked a bit like a giant wooden seesaw with – instead of a seat – a saucer-shaped platform for loading boulders onto. The other end of the room had a mini Roman bath, with a changing room hung with togas, and a round, high-sided pool filled with water. In between was a mosaic floor, and a table with a fake banquet, including piles of plastic grapes and a plateful of cardboard chickens.

The crowd had been ushered in and was standing in a roped-off area to one side of the room. Behind the rows of autograph-hunters, Stuart could see his father, and also a grey-haired man with a large black moustache: Maxwell Lacey, Miss Edie's lawyer. He was looking directly at Stuart.

'Welcome, everybody,' said Rod Felton, stepping onto a small stage at the catapult end of the room, and speaking (much too loudly) into a microphone. 'Or should I say,' he added, with the expression of someone about to tell a joke, 'Amici, Romani, Cives?'

Stuart's father (and only Stuart's father) laughed heartily. Everyone turned to look at him.

'As chief curator,' Rod continued, 'I'd like to say a few words about all the incredibly hard work and intense research that has gone into mounting this marvellous exhibition, so before I introduce our special—'

There was the clatter of heels as Rowena Allsopp suddenly appeared on the stage. She was wearing a bright orange suit with metal buttons that gleamed like gold coins, and she was waving at the audience.

'Oh,' said Rod, 'I was just—'

'Hello, *Beeton*!' called Rowena Allsopp, taking the microphone from him. A camera flashed, and Stuart saw that it belonged to May, who was crouching in front of the stage.

'It's so *lovely* to see so many of my *wonderful* fans here on this very, *very* special occasion – the unique *chance* to view some of my favourite *outfits*, which are on display in a room just down the *corridor* from this one, followed by an opportunity to purchase *signed* copies of my very own auto*bio*graphy – and there's an exciting *discount* if you buy more than *three* copies. I just can't wait to meet you *all*!'

She gave the microphone back to a stunned-looking Rod Felton. He cleared his throat and leaned across to her.

'The Roman Beeton exhibition?' he whispered plaintively.

'Oh yes.' Rowena grabbed the microphone back again. 'I now declare this exhibition open,' she announced briskly and unenthusiastically.

May's camera flashed several times in succession, and Rowena smiled and posed, blinking glassily in the brilliant light. 'That's enough,' she ordered after a minute or so. 'I can't see a thing,' and she tottered off the stage towards the exit.

'Mind the ballista!' called Rod.

'The whatsit?' said Rowena, looking round irritably and walking straight beyond a sign that read: CAUTION – DO NOT WALK BEYOND THIS SIGN.

'The *ballista*,' repeated Rod.

'For heaven's sake, why can't you speak Eng—?'

The photographs of what happened next ended up on the front page of every newspaper in the country. They resulted in record-breaking numbers of visitors to the Roman Beeton exhibition and eventually led to May getting a special junior prize in the European News Photo-Journalism Action Sequence of the Year awards.

They were as follows:

Photo 1 showed Rowena tripping over one of her heels;

Photo 2 showed her sitting down heavily on a saucer-shaped wooden platform;

Photo 3 showed her struggling to get up, and grabbing at what looked like a convenient lever;

Photo 4 showed her being catapulted through the air like a giant gold-and-orange firework; and

Photo 5 showed her landing, with a massive splash, in the circular Roman bath at the far end of the room.

What the pictures didn't convey was the disbelieving silence that blanketed the room as Rowena struggled to her feet in the waist-high water. For a moment she seemed too shocked to speak, and simply stood, mouth open, hair like dank seaweed, jacket sodden, buttons half hanging off. And then the silence was broken by one of her golden buttons dropping into the pool with a teeny tiny splish. Like a coin dropping into a fountain.

'Make a wish,' said someone at the back of the crowd.

There was a smothered giggle, and then Rod Felton rushed forward and everyone started talking and squawking and shrieking at once. Everyone except Stuart, who stood as if rooted; in his head, an idea was beginning to grow.

'Throw in a coin and make a wish,' he muttered to himself. 'Make a *wish*.' And then his eyes widened, and he turned and grabbed April's shoulder and said, 'I've got it.'

'What?'

'Where the will is. Come *on*!' And he turned and ran out of the room and along the corridor and down into the basement, April at his heels.

'The one place we didn't think of . . .' he said, panting. 'The trick we forgot about . . . the illusion it all started with. And Miss Edie gave us the clue, remember? She said the will was well hidden. Do you get it?'

The shabby cluster of tricks lay before them. 'Here, help me move this,' said Stuart, tugging at the Fan of Fantasticality.

Together, they slid it to one side. Behind, fully visible now, was the Well of Wishes, and April laughed with sudden realization. 'You're right,' she said. 'Well hidden. This is the place.'

Chapter 41

They stood on either side of the Well of Wishes. Scraped and battered it may have been, but it was still beautiful, steeped in shadow, dusted with the sparkle of stars.

'And what else did Miss Edie say?' asked April.

'*Use the male. Use the male to find it.*' Stuart could almost hear Miss Edie's rasping transatlantic voice.

April stared thoughtfully into the well, and then she gave a squeak and leaned further forward. 'I can see something,' she said.

Stuart craned over the parapet. Just visible was a series of spidery copper letters, evenly spaced around the inside of the well.

'It's says something,' said April, almost upside down. 'It says . . . hang on . . . it says PLACED WHERE IT SHALL BE FOUND. Or it might be WHERE IT SHALL BE FOUND PLACED. All the spaces between the letters are the same.'

She straightened up, her face flushed. 'I don't understand,' she said. 'How can those words help us? Either way round.'

And Stuart was just about to shrug when the answer came to him, quick and complete and whole. 'It's not the words that count,' he said.

'What?'

'When Miss Edie said *Use the mail to help you*, she didn't mean M-A-L-E, she meant M-A-I-L! What we call post. And what do you get in the mail? Not words but—'

'Letters!' shouted April.

'And the clues we got were letters,' he said. 'SWOTIE.'

Together, they leaned over the parapet again. The copper letters seemed to glow softly.

PLACEDWHEREITSHALLBEFOUND

Stuart reached out his hand and touched the S of SHALL. The copper letter was slightly raised. He pressed, and it moved inwards with a delicate *click*.

Without speaking, April reached out for the W and did the same thing.

One by one, turn by turn, they touched the letters – O, T, I – and then April paused, arm outstretched.

'There are *four* Es,' she said. 'Which one should I press?'

They straightened up and looked at each other.

'It *was* definitely E in the last illusion, wasn't it?' asked April.

Stuart started to say yes and then stopped. 'I had to find the right world in the Book of Peril,' he said. '*My* right world. **A** had my wrong dad, and so did **B**. **C** was – well, **C** just wasn't right, **D** was my wrong mum and **E**...' He hesitated, and then spoke more quietly.

'**E** was the wrong me. A taller me. I shouldn't really have chosen **E** at all, I should have gone further, only I was afraid we'd get stuck there.'

'And we nearly did,' said April. 'So thank goodness you did choose it. But that means the last letter isn't an E – it could be *any* letter further along in the alphabet. So which one should I press? N? Or P? Or T? T for Tony?'

'Or F,' suggested Stuart. 'F for final. F for finish.'

'F for friendship,' said April. 'I think that's the one we should try. Don't you?'

Stuart nodded, and April leaned back over the parapet and pressed the letter. With a sound like a gentle sigh, a section of the parapet slid aside, leaving a hole the size and shape of a letter box.

They both peered into it.

'Go on, then,' urged April, giving Stuart a bossy nudge. 'It's yours.'

Stuart started to lift his hand, and then he stopped. He thought of April shouting advice to him in the Arch of Mirrors. He thought of her working out how to operate the Reappearing Rose Bower. He thought of her running unhesitatingly back into danger to find Charlie.

'No,' he said. 'It's not just mine.'

'What?'

'It wouldn't be fair. I couldn't ever have got this far by myself.'

April looked puzzled, and then – as his meaning dawned on her – her eyes widened. 'Do you really mean it?' she asked.

'I mean it,' said Stuart. 'We *both* get the will. One. Two. *Three.*'

Together they reached into the letter box, and together their fingers touched a papery cylinder and drew it out. It was tied with a length of red string, and April untangled the knot, and Stuart smoothed out the paper. It was headed:

LAST WILL AND TESTAMENT OF ANTHONY HORTEN

and was followed by half a page of handwriting, all long, convoluted sentences stuffed with complex words.

'Complicated, isn't it?' muttered Stuart.

'May I see?' asked another voice behind them.

They spun round and saw Maxwell Lacey.

'Because if you've found a will, then I really would advise you to consult a lawyer,' he said, holding out his hand. 'I guarantee that my current service will be free of charge.'

Stuart looked at April and she shrugged. 'Might as well,' she said. '*We* can't make head nor tail of it.'

Maxwell Lacey read the document carefully and then let it snap into a cylinder again before handing it back.

'Straightforward,' he said. 'And fully legal. In essence, the discoverer of the will is the owner of the magical illusions – finders keepers, in other words.'

'Ours to keep,' said Stuart, his mouth curving into a grin. 'And ours to sell.'

'Indeed,' agreed Maxwell Lacey. 'And I'm sure my client's offer will be to your joint satisfaction. I shall, of course, have to speak to your respective parents, who would be advised to take financial advice of their own, but in the case of—'

'Excuse me?' said April, putting up her hand. 'Can I ask something?'

'Go ahead, young lady.'

'I'm just being curious, but what's Miss Edie actually going to *do* with the illusions?'

For the first time, Maxwell Lacey appeared disconcerted. He paused, and appeared to choose his words. 'I believe that she has a specific destination in mind for them.'

'You mean a museum or something?'

'No, I don't think a museum is part of her plans.'

There was a pause. Stuart looked at April, and then back at Mr Lacey. 'What do you mean, a *destination*?' he asked.

The lawyer gave a short sigh. 'My client's grandmother, Jean Carr, was a shrewd businesswoman with a particular interest in the invention and manufacture of stage tricks. She emigrated from England to Canada and founded a huge and successful industry.'

'We know,' said April and Stuart simultaneously.

'You do? Well, with a portion of her frankly enormous fortune, she had a statue of herself erected outside the factory she owned, with a space underneath for a large metal plaque, detailing her remarkable life and achievements. Some eighty years after her death, the space for that plaque remains empty.'

'Why?'

'Because apparently – and I have no explanation for how this is possible – she wished for it to be manufactured from a very specific metallic source.' He cleared his throat and his gaze slid past Stuart towards the objects behind him.

Stuart caught his breath. 'Great-Uncle Tony's tricks,' he said. 'She wanted these tricks found and then melted down and made into the plaque!'

Maxwell Lacey nodded stiffly. 'That is correct. And that is precisely my client's intention.'

'But that's such a *waste*,' exclaimed April. 'A waste of money and a waste of *things* – these tricks are fantastic, they're unique.'

'It's Jeannie Carr's revenge,' said Stuart, with

utter certainty. 'If she couldn't have them, then she wanted to make sure that nobody else ever could.'

He felt suddenly protective of the shabby cluster of illusions. They didn't *deserve* to be squashed and ruined; they should be cherished, he thought. Cherished and used. He remembered the strange feeling he'd had of being on a bridge: on one side of him a heap of cash, on the other the world of illusion and adventure conjured up by his great-uncle.

April had her hand up again.

'Yes?' asked Maxwell Lacey.

'Why did you tell us?'

'Excuse me?'

'Why did you tell us what Miss Edie was going to do with the tricks? Did you have to? Legally, I mean?'

The lawyer's eyebrows shot up in surprise. 'Ever thought of becoming a lawyer yourself?' he asked.

'Yes,' said April.

'OK, well then – no, I didn't have to tell you.'

'So why did you?'

'Because I happen to agree with you that it's a waste. I think Miss Edie could do a whole lot of charitable good with the money she possesses, instead of spending it on some kind of ancient score-settling that I don't happen to understand. However, as her lawyer, I am obliged to carry out her current wishes.'

'Yes, but *we're* not,' said Stuart.

'No,' echoed April. 'And if we don't agree to sell them, then maybe she'll spend her cash on something better.'

A small smile appeared on Maxwell Lacey's pale, composed face. 'You would be turning down a life-changing amount of money.'

'My life's already changed,' said Stuart.

'And I don't know that I want to change my life *that* much,' said April. 'I already argue with my sisters most of the time. Imagine the arguments we'd have if I was the only millionaire in the family. And anyway, I'd rather become a millionaire by doing something brilliant and useful.'

Maxwell Lacey nodded. 'Yes, I can see that

happening,' he said drily. 'And you,' he asked Stuart. 'Will you become a stage magician like your great-uncle?'

Stuart tried to imagine himself standing in a spotlight in front of a huge, expectant audience, and hastily shook his head. 'I think I'd rather do something adventurous. Outdoors. Crossing deserts on camels, mapping out uncharted territories.'

'Bravely rescuing people who've got stuck,' added April, nudging him.

'Yes, that sort of thing,' he said, a bit embarrassed.

'So what will you do with Tony Horten's legacy,' asked the lawyer, 'if you don't sell it to my client?'

All three of them turned to look at the illusions, and Stuart thought of his great-uncle's message:

LETTERS, AND WHEN YOU HAVE ALL SIX, THEY'LL
LEAD YOU TO MY W   OU CAN DECIDE IF YOU
TRULY WISH TO K   RHAPS GIVE THEM
AWAY TO SO

The Well of Wishes, the Pharaoh's Pyramid,

the Arch of Mirrors, the Fan of Fantasticality, the Reappearing Rose Bower, the Cabinet of Blood, the Book of Peril: seven miracles of engineering, seven gateways to magical worlds (now closed for ever), seven tricks in need of skilled and loving attention and an admiring audience.

'I've got an idea,' said Stuart.

Epilogue

'See you tomorrow then, Stuey,' shouted one of Stuart's friends as he turned the corner into Beech Road.

'See you.'

It was a crisply cold day in November, the sky a brilliant blue, and Stuart was just arriving home from school. Everyone in his new class called him 'Stuey' and he quite liked it. It was certainly no worse than anyone else's nickname, and a lot, lot better than Shorty Shorten. No one ever called him *that* any more.

'Hail,' said his father. 'Another satisfactory day at your pedagogic institution?'

'Yeah, it was pretty good,' replied Stuart.

'And how was the inaugural meeting of the

after-school Explorer's Club?'

'All right. In fact I've, er . . . I've been voted president of it. Unanimously.' He tried to sound casual, but it was hard not to show how pleased he was.

His father smiled. 'Splendid.'

'Dad, can I go round to April's after supper? She's writing an article on dog-training for the school magazine and we want to try and teach Charlie to balance a biscuit on his nose.'

Although what Stuart *really* wished he could teach the dog was to come when he was called. He opened the back door and tried out another couple of names he'd thought of on the way home.

'Chuckle! Chopper!' The dog carried on sniffing round the garden.

'A duo of postal missives arrived for you,' said his father.

'Two letters? For me?'

The first was a large envelope with a cluster of Canadian stamps. Stuart opened it and drew out a rectangle of cream card, edged in gold.

YOU ARE CORDIALLY INVITED
TO A GRAND RECEPTION TO
CELEBRATE THE OPENING OF THE

**JEANNIE CARR
CHARITABLE FOUNDATION
'WELL OF WISHES' PROJECT**

A SCHEME TO PROVIDE CLEAN
DRINKING WATER TO POORER
COMMUNITIES ACROSS THE WORLD

ALSO INCORPORATING THE JEANNIE CARR CHARITABLE
FOUNDATION 'GOOD MANNERS' PROJECT, A SCHEME TO
MAKE MODERN CHILDREN MORE RESPECTFUL AND
LESS DISOBEDIENT TO THEIR ELDERS.

Grinning, Stuart turned the card over and saw a
few lines of handwriting.

Dear Stuart and April,

I would imagine that you're unlikely to be able to attend this event, given that it's in Toronto, so I will therefore be unable to thank you in person. You should be proud, however, of the results of your decision not to sell the tricks — rather than wasting her fortune on empty revenge, my client is at last doing something useful with her grandmother's money. Well done to the pair of you, and good luck — now and in the future.

Cordially,
Maxwell Lacey

The other envelope contained a small object wrapped in tissue paper, a newspaper cutting and a postcard of a theatre, with a cheerfully scrawled pencil message on the back.

DON'T KNOW IF YOU SAW THIS - BEST REVIEW I'VE EVER HAD! THERE WAS ALSO A TALENT SCOUT IN THE AUDIENCE, AND ELAINE AND I HAVE NOW GOT

A FIVE-WEEK RUN AS THE PALACE
CONJURERS IN 'SLEEPING BEAUTY' AT
SOUTHEND-ON-SEA THEATRE ROYAL. ALL
THANKS TO YOU AND APRIL!
COME AND SEE US!
CLIFFORD.
P.S. GETTING MARRIED IN JANUARY.

P.P.S. ELAINE FOUND THIS THING WHEN
SHE WAS RENOVATING THE WELL OF
WISHES – IT WAS IN THE SAME SPACE
THAT YOU FOUND THE WILL. HOPE IT'S
USEFUL.

Stuart picked up the small object wrapped in tissue paper. He could feel through the wrapping that it was small and circular. *It's a coin*, he thought, and then drew a quick breath.

A coin.

A coin that had been found in the Well of Wishes.

He gripped the object, not knowing quite how he felt – anxious? Scared? Excited? Could this, he wondered, be the start of a whole new quest? He hesitated for a long moment before putting it down again, still wrapped, and unfolding the cutting from the *Beech Road Guardian*.

TRIUMPH!

Those members of the audience who had seen Mysterioso the Magician's first two shows were rewarded for their loyalty last week with his triumphant third outing, in which the wonders of the lighting were actually matched by the fabulousness of the magic tricks themselves.

GASPS!!

Audience members gasped in amazement as a series of incredible illusions took place before their very eyes. Mysterioso's lovely assistant Elaine, in an elegant silver boiler-suit, survived being impaled with swords, trapped in a pyramid and shut into a giant book, and when an entire arch made of mirrors completely disappeared, there was a standing ovation which went on for nearly a minute.

DONATION!!

After the show, Mysterioso (also known as Mr Clifford Capstone) publicly thanked his young friends April Kingley (10) and Stuart Horten (also 10) for their kind donation of the tricks, which had originally been created nearly fifty years ago by the extraordinary and brilliant magician known as Teeny-tiny Tony Horten. Mysterioso also thanked his assistant, Elaine Coleridge, for her skilled restoration of the previously somewhat battered illusions, which now looked as good as new. Finally he thanked his guinea pig, Gerald, for

'Stuart!'

April was standing at the back fence, pointing at her watch and then holding up a dog biscuit.

'TEN MINUTES!' shouted Stuart through the window. 'I WANT SOMETHING TO EAT FIRST.'

'OK.'

Stuart glanced at Clifford's postcard again, and then, for the second time, picked up the tissue-wrapped coin. Quickly, before he could lose his nerve, he unwrapped it.

A small metal disc fell out, bounced on the table top and then rolled to a stop.

Relief and disappointment mingled inside him, and he found himself laughing.

It *wasn't* a coin.

It had a hole punched through it and a name etched in capitals across both sides. A short name. A short name for a short dog.

Stuart ran to the back door and wrenched it open.

'Chips!' he shouted.

And Chips came running.

THE END